THE SWEET PART

KYLIE GILMORE

Cover design by: Sweet 'N Spicy Designs

Published by: Extra Fancy Books

ISBN-13: 978-1-64658-131-3

1

———

May

Sometimes you just need a share-size bag of M&M's all to yourself.

I pop a handful of M&M's into my mouth and step out of my house into the crisp winter air of Clover Park, Connecticut. Thankfully, my secret chocolate stash on the high shelf of the pantry has yet to be discovered by my five-year-old daughter, Sophie. I left her with my twin sister, Alice, so I can clear my head.

It's a few days after a stressful Christmas, where Sophie burst into tears because Santa didn't bring her secret Christmas wish. If only I'd known what she wanted, I could've explained that our little family is complete. And she has my parents, sister, aunts, uncles, and cousins living nearby. She just won't let it go.

Maybe a puppy?

I drain the remainder of the M&M bag into my mouth. *Am I nuts? A puppy is not the answer.* Our house is already chaos with the whirlwind that is Sophie and the renovations to turn my old Victorian home into an inn. Serenity Inn because I long for serenity. One day.

I stroll along Main Street, taking in the white lights twinkling in decorative arches over the street. More white lights wrap along the trees that line both sides of the street. I love Clover Park. I grew up here and moved back because I wanted Sophie to have the same experience I did living here. It's a quaint small town centered around Main Street with shops and restaurants, a few churches, historic Ludbury House, a library, and Baldwin Park. Farther out from town, you'll find miles of wooded rolling hills dotted with ponds and streams. Just beautiful, even in winter.

I reach the front door of Happy Endings, our local bar with its cheerful red sign, and stop. A glass of red wine would go nicely with the sugar high from mainlining M&M's. I step inside, and warmth envelops me instantly like a hug. This place is dear to my heart. My grandparents used to own it, and I spent a lot of time here as a kid. To my right is the restaurant area with a lively crowd. The space is decorated with cheerful balloons and streamers. Must be a party of some kind.

Straight ahead is my destination—a dark cherrywood bar. The new owner added a large room onto the back of the place with a dance floor, vintage jukebox, and pool tables. After a glass of wine, maybe I'll dance like no one's watching. Ha! I'll be lucky to have the energy to sit on a bar stool. It's tough to be a working single mom.

Not that I'm complaining. I love Sophie more than anyone in the world, including my twin. (Don't tell Alice I said that.) And the old Victorian I'm renovating as an inn is a gift inherited from my great-grandmother Maggie. With Sophie in school full-time, it seemed like the timing was right to start my own business.

Besides, the house was too big for just the two of us, and Alice and I didn't want to sell our inheritance. When I came up with the idea for how to keep it in the family, Alice sold her share to me. Well, I'm still paying her back, but we have a payment plan. If the inn is successful, I'll be able to pay her, clear the renovation debt, and support me and Sophie going forward. No pressure!

I do have my husband's life insurance payout in a savings

account, but I don't want to dip into it too much. My plan is for the bulk of it to go toward Sophie's college tuition.

I take a seat at the bar and spot a waiter circulating with champagne. Then I hear someone asking to see the ring. Oops. I think I stumbled into an engagement party. But there was no sign on the door saying closed for a private event.

I take a seat and smile at the bartender, Cooper Campbell. He's the son of the owner. "I didn't know I walked into an engagement party."

"It's okay, May," Cooper says. "Still open to the public. What can I get you?"

He knew it was me and not my identical twin. That's nice. Not many people can tell the difference. It's easy if you know us. Alice is the stylish, put-together one. I'm the frazzled one.

"Points for the right name," I say. "A glass of merlot, please."

He inclines his head and pours the merlot, handing it to me.

"Last one, I promise," he says to a beautiful brunette woman standing just behind me. I glance at her hand with a shiny diamond engagement ring. Is this Cooper's engagement party? And he's working?

A tall dark-haired man leans across the bar next to me to clap Cooper on the shoulder. He's gorgeous with thick lashes, high cheekbones, and a square jaw. He's close enough I can see the dark stubble on his jaw. A hot flash fires through my body. *I'm not old enough for hot flashes!* He looks familiar, but I don't know why.

"What're you doing working behind the bar?" the familiar, gorgeous man says to Cooper. "Get out here. I'll do that." He goes behind the bar.

Our gazes collide when he faces me, his deep brown eyes meeting mine, and then he gives me a sexy smile that sends a low throb in a place that hasn't throbbed in quite a long time. For a man, anyway. My vibrator doesn't count.

Suddenly I know why he looks familiar. It's Mason Shaw. "I know you! You're that guy on *Hot Finds*. I love that show."

Hot Finds is this fun show where they restore a classic car and sell it at auction. Mason hosts it. I swear he must have women across the country tuning in just to see him, imagining he's talking to them in that deep voice. Not me, of course. It's the easy banter between father and son that got me hooked. His dad explains the technical stuff.

Okay, I'm a total Mason fangirl.

Mason leans an elbow on the bar, getting close enough for his clean scent to wash over me. My pulse spikes. "That's me. Cool that you watch the show. We have mostly a male demographic."

"You're even more good looking in person." I slap a hand over my mouth, horrified. "I can't believe I said that out loud."

"Say whatever you want. I love to hear it. I'm Mason."

"I know." I laugh. "I'm May. My grandparents used to own this place. Back then it was called Garner's Sports Bar & Grill."

"Is that right? Well, I'm glad you walked in today, May."

"Me too." I could drown in those brown eyes. Like a vat of chocolate.

"Another *M* name. Lot of those in my family. My three younger brothers have names that start with an *M*, two of my cousins, and my mom." The easy charm he shows on TV translates in real life at ten times the intensity. A hundred times.

"And now you met another *M*, me."

"May, you're the prettiest one of them all."

I suck in air and quickly cover. "I hope so if you're comparing me to your brothers!" My voice hits a high note that would normally embarrass me, but he laughs, and I find myself laughing too.

"Mommy! Mommy!"

Sophie runs straight to me, her pigtails askew as usual. I scoop her up, relaxing with my baby in my arms once more. "Did you have fun with Aunt Alice?"

She nods enthusiastically.

Alice gives me an apologetic look. Her long light brown hair shines. What a pretty color, almost caramel. Guess I'm complimenting myself too. Ha. Alice looks stylish as ever wearing an off-the-shoulder wine red sweater, gray skinny jeans, and long leather boots. It's laundry day at my house, so I'm wearing a pink T-shirt that shrank in the wash, revealing a stripe of skin on my stomach that I keep trying to cover by pulling up my navy, ankle-length skirt. It's a summer skirt, really. I threw on a gray cardigan for warmth and bam! Fashion mom. Not.

"Sorry," Alice says. "I kept her distracted as long as I could."

Mason stares at Sophie and then me, surprise registering on his face.

"Single mom," I say, setting Sophie down.

He shifts uncomfortably. That's *fine*. I'm not in dating mode. I was just enjoying meeting a local celebrity. He glances quickly between me and Alice, noticing we're identical. We get that a lot.

Sophie grabs my arm. "Mommy, that's Mason from *Hot Finds*!" She turns to him. "Can I get your autograph?"

He smiles. "Sure." Grabbing a napkin, he looks around for a pen. I fish one out of my purse and hand it to him. "Thanks."

Alice elbows me, whispering, "Now I get why you watch a car show."

I give her a warning look that says *drop it!* I have to be extra careful not to show interest in men when Sophie's around. Made that mistake before.

Mason turns to Sophie. "Who should I make it out to?"

She cocks her head. "Huh?"

He leans down. "What's your name?"

"Sophie Herman. I live at—"

I put a hand on her shoulder. "We don't share our address with everyone."

"But I know it!"

"Just Sophie's good," Mason says. He writes on the napkin, using his other hand to shield what he's writing.

Sophie goes on tiptoe, trying to see it.

When he finishes, he presents the napkin with a flourish.

"Wow," she says in a hushed tone.

Alice and I lean over, trying to read it. Sophie can read thanks to me.

"Lemme see," I tell Sophie. She holds the napkin up. He wrote: Sophie, ride on! Mason. At the bottom of the napkin, he made a drawing of a sports car with fins.

She hugs it to her chest. "Wait until I show Olivia H.! Can I be on your TV show?"

I frown. "Sophie, Mason was very generous to give you his autograph and this nice drawing. Don't keep asking him for things."

She clasps her hands together, careful to keep the napkin flat between them. "Ple-eeze, ple-eeze, ple-eeze."

So not happy with the begging. I'm about to say we need to go when Mason says, "We only film in the spring. Sorry. The rest of the time I'm just a boring mechanic."

"Spring comes after winter," she tells me. "It's winter, spring, summer, fall, winter, over and over." She turns to him and says proudly, "I know my seasons, how to write my name, and I can read."

"Whoa!" he says.

She nods vigorously. "I've been reading since I was three. Sometimes I read to my class at circle time."

"Now that's impressive." He actually sounds sincere.

She preens and tosses her pigtails back over her shoulders. "I'm going to learn to ride a bike soon. Mommy says in the spring, so that's two things I'm doing in the spring. The other one is Easter." She throws her arms wide. "I can't wait for spring!"

"Exciting stuff," he says. "Easter Bunny and all that."

She glances at me before telling him, "If I don't get what I want for my birthday, I'll ask the Easter Bunny."

"Or the Tooth Fairy," he says.

She puts her signed napkin on the bar and tries to climb onto a stool. I give her a boost. "What's the Tooth Fairy do?"

He checks in with me, and I incline my head. "When you get a loose tooth, it'll eventually come out. Then you put the tooth under your pillow, and the Tooth Fairy takes it and leaves you money." I hold up one finger behind her back. "Like a dollar."

Sophie covers her mouth. "But I like my teeth."

"It's just the baby teeth that come out," I reassure her. "That's to make room for your bigger, grown-up teeth. Like mine."

I bare my teeth at her to show her my big teeth. Mason and Alice do too.

Sophie gazes at Mason adoringly. "You know everything. When I blow out the candles on my birthday cake, I'm gonna wish for *you* to be my daddy."

Mason's jaw drops. I freeze, mortified.

"Oh boy," Alice says under her breath.

"Sophie, we should get back home," I say. "It's getting late."

"I have to go to the bathroom," she announces, leaning toward me with her arms outstretched. I help her down from the bar stool, and she dashes to the ladies' room.

"I'll go with her," Alice says, sending me a sympathetic look.

He glances around, jerking his chin at an older man looking at us. Oh, it's his dad, Parker Shaw. Mason continues looking everywhere but at me.

I give him a wry smile. "Santa didn't bring her a daddy, so I guess she's moved on to the next holiday. Next she'll write a letter to the Easter Bunny." I laugh, trying to make light of it.

He doesn't laugh.

I get serious. "Her dad died when she was two. She doesn't remember him."

"Oh, I'm sorry."

"Thanks." I carefully put Sophie's autographed napkin in my purse and toss back the rest of my wine. "I guess she feels left out now that she's in kindergarten and found out all her friends have dads." I sigh. "When she realized she was the only one who didn't, she decided to do something about it. She's very persistent."

He nods.

I exhale sharply. "Anyway, I don't date, so she just has to get her head around the fact that a daddy isn't a gift that magically appears."

He leans closer, and I get a hot flash. *I swear I'm too young for hot flashes!* "Why don't you date?"

My brain stalls. I smooth my hair back, flustered by his close attention, his deep brown eyes, his sexiness. *Think, May, why don't you date?* "I have a young impressionable daughter, and I'm too busy getting my new inn ready to open."

And I'm afraid to fall in love again. It feels like a betrayal of my husband. I did try dating. Once. Last year I saw a guy from work casually. I made the mistake of letting Sophie meet him, and she got attached. When I discovered he was cheating, it was easy to let him go. Sophie was devastated when it was over. That's more than enough reasons to swear off men.

At Mason's continued closeness, and my continued heart-pounding, flushed excitement, I look around the room. *Excitement? Yikes!* "Is Cooper still here?"

"What do you need him for?"

"My handyman broke his arm, and I haven't had much luck finding help during the holidays. I hoped Cooper might be available for a few minor repairs at the inn."

"Anything my cousin can do, I can do better."

My gaze snaps to his. "Well, it's not a contest."

He grins. "What do you need?"

"A deer knocked down part of the deer fence in the back-yard—" I pantomime a deer leaping over the fence "—also I need some drywall repair in the guest bedrooms, and someone to install new light fixtures. I can't get the electrician back for six weeks. I want to finish soon so I can get pictures for the website and marketing materials. I'm planning to open Valentine's Day weekend."

One corner of his mouth lifts in a sexy smile, making my pulse race alarmingly. "Consider it done. I'm all yours."

My hand flutters in the air. "No, never mind. I'll find someone. I'm sure you're very busy with work and your TV show."

"May, I can do it. I have off this week. I'll work on it the day after New Year's Eve. That'll give me four days and—"

"But that's your vacation time."

He tucks his hands in his trouser pockets. "Between my dad and uncles, I'm well trained. Trust me, I'm good with my hands."

I pull my collar away from my neck, desperately trying to cool off. *Is Mason Shaw flirting with me?*

He brushes his hands together. "Done deal."

I focus on his broad chest, forcing myself to think this through.

He's capable. I've seen him fix cars on TV. This work is probably much easier for him.

He's available right away.

He's gorgeous, but you can't hold that against the guy.

It's crunch time for the inn. If I have any hope of opening on Valentine's Day weekend, I need to get this work done. Then I can get the word out to make the inn a success, support my family, pay off my debts. You know, all that crucial adulting stuff.

"Thank you," I say.

He inclines his head, seeming pleased by my acceptance of his generous offer.

"I'll pay you, of course. I just need…" I trail off as he crooks his finger at me. I swallow hard and lean in.

His voice turns husky. "I'll do it for free if you let me buy you a drink sometime. Just a drink, no pressure."

That sounds like a seduction scene in the making. Before I can answer a cheerful thanks, but that's not necessary, small hands grab the back of my cardigan. "I have to dry my hands," Sophie chirps, using my cardigan to complete the job.

I look at her over my shoulder. "Why didn't you use the dryer in the bathroom?"

"It's the new kind that looks like a hand trap." She must mean the kind of dryer you stick your hands into for air.

I pull her out from behind me. "Next time dry your hands on your own shirt."

"But then my shirt will get wet."

Mason chuckles.

"I told her to shake her hands in the air," Alice says. She kisses my cheek and gives Sophie a hug. "Bye, ladies! Bye, Mason. Nice to meet you."

He raises a hand. "You too, uh, May's twin."

"Alice," she supplies helpfully. "May was too dazzled by your presence to introduce me earlier."

"Shut up," I say under my breath.

Alice wiggles her fingers and sails out the door.

I blow out a breath and give Mason a quick smile. "I was distracted by Sophie. That's why I forgot to introduce Alice."

He lifts his brows. "Mmm-hmm. Have you and Alice ever pulled the twin switcheroo?"

"Not since high school."

"My twin brothers love to trade places. And my uncle Josh and uncle Jake, also identical, pulled a switcheroo on the women they ultimately married."

I can feel myself getting sucked in, wanting to know more, but I have Sophie here with me.

"That sounds like a story for another time," I say. "Unfortunately, we have to go. Thanks again, and I'll pay you, okay?" *No seduction here.* I take Sophie by her damp hand and turn to go.

"Where's your inn?" he asks.

I stop and turn back. That would be good info to share. I give him the address.

"I know where that is. If it's all right, I'll stop by tomorrow to get an idea of what I'll need to bring for repairs."

I nod. *Tomorrow. A gorgeous repairman. That'll be a first. Ooh! Maybe I can put him in the brochure!*

"You're coming to my house?" Sophie exclaims excitedly.

He smiles. "You bet."

She jumps up and down. "Yay!"

I sober. I don't want Sophie getting attached to a guy who won't be sticking around for long.

I hurry her toward the door, saying a brief goodbye over my shoulder.

"Mommy, you shared our address," Sophie says accusingly. "You said we don't share our address with everyone."

"I know, but it's because he's going to fix things for the inn."

Sophie chatters on excitedly about Mason visiting, and how she wants to show him all the stuffed animals in her room.

Four days, that's all. I'll compensate him somehow. That will make it a simple business transaction. No complications. No broken little-girl hearts. A drink for free repairs is not how I roll. I know how guys think. A drink, back to his place, ba-da-boom—one-night stand.

I've never had a one-night stand in my life, and I don't intend to start now.

I push the front door open, relieved by the blast of cold winter air for my overheated body. He's just another repairman.

This is no problem. Really.

2

Mason

I pull a pink note off the windshield of my black Ford F-150 pickup truck, scan it quickly, and crumple it up. This superfan I met *once* at Happy Endings bar won't leave me alone. She keeps leaving her number, asking me to call because it's IMPORTANT. I should probably get a restraining order, but so far she's just left notes on my windshield and showed up at Exotic and Classic Restorations, where I work. My coworkers do a good job keeping her away from me.

I scan the parking lot of the pizzeria, where I grabbed a quick bite. I don't see Evie. I hope she left the note and went on her way. The fact that the pizzeria is close to my house gives me pause. It's possible she followed me here from home. My address is just a quick internet search away.

If she shows up at my house, I'll tell her I'm not interested, and if she keeps trying to connect with me, then I'll file a restraining order. That settled, I get in the truck and put her out of my mind. I'm heading to May's future inn to take a look around.

There's something about May. Yes, she's beautiful with her caramel brown hair and sparkling hazel eyes, but I also loved her laugh, her sweet demeanor, her sexy midriff top. I was way into that glimpse of bare skin before her daughter arrived. That was a shock. May's a single mom, and she was crystal clear that she doesn't date.

Still, I couldn't help but offer to get a drink with her in exchange for the repairs. I don't expect her to take me up on it, and I won't ask again. I respect her boundaries.

I just wish I could stop thinking about her.

Even her identical twin couldn't pull my attention away. A different energy. I puzzle over that. Two equally beautiful women, but I'm only attracted to one. Sweet and sexy does it for me, I guess.

A short while later, I park and walk up the front walk of May's future inn. I've seen the place before when I was in town to visit my cousins, who live across the street. It's a classic Victorian, white with black shutters and a wraparound porch.

Sophie has her nose pressed against a front window, watching me approach. I wave. She waves, throws the curtain back, and races away. Guess she's setting off the alarm that the famous Mason Shaw is here. I started hosting *Hot Finds* a couple of years back when my uncle Ty stepped down for a new venture in community wellness programs. Anyway, fans of the show are mostly guys who want to shake my hand. Yesterday was my first time signing an autograph for a pint-size fan.

The front door opens, and Sophie steps out on the porch, barefoot in a purple dress with green corduroy pants underneath. "Come in!"

I jog up the front steps since it's cold out, and Sophie's barefoot.

May appears behind her. "Sophie! Get inside; it's freezing out here! And put on socks and slippers like I told you to."

"My feet aren't cold," Sophie protests, kicking her feet behind her in a little jig. "See?"

May speaks between her teeth. "Now, please."

"But Mason's here!"

"I only hang out with people wearing socks and slippers."

She dashes off just as I step inside, brushing by May. Mmm, she smells like vanilla. "Hi."

She shuts the door. "Hi. Thanks for coming."

No cardigan and midriff T-shirt today. She's in a light blue clingy sweater and leggings. Still sexy.

She gestures around her. "So, this is it."

I take in the gleaming hardwood floors of the front entryway leading into the living room. A fireplace with a white carved mantel and brick surround looks original to the house. The furniture isn't formal like I imagined a Victorian home would have. Instead there's two comfy-looking dark green sofas and oversized red velvet chairs. No TV.

Sophie appears at the top of the stairs and holds out a foot. "Look! I'm wearing socks and Crocs. Mason, come to my room!"

I turn to May, not sure how to respond. Sophie probably wants to show me her toys, but I'm here for a job. Besides, May might not want me to be alone with her daughter. We just met, after all. She doesn't know I'm trustworthy.

"She wants to show you her stuffed animal collection," May says. "We'll do that on the way to the other bedrooms. We live on the third floor, guests are on the second, communal area on the first floor."

I walk with her upstairs. "What's the name of your inn?"

"Serenity Inn."

"Interesting."

"I'm having a sign made. Anyway, it's a reminder to myself to find serenity amid the chaos, and I hope it'll attract guests seeking serenity too."

"Are you going to have a spa? That's what I think of when I hear serenity."

"Up here!" Sophie shouts.

"We'd better check out her stuffed animals first, or she'll hound you. No plans for a spa, but it's a good idea. Maybe down the line we'll offer massages. Add that to my long list of potential items for the inn."

We get to the third floor, and May opens a door leading to

stairs. We can hear Sophie banging around up there. I gesture for May to go first because I'm a gentleman.

I follow May and keep my eyes glued to her shapely ass. Kidding. I only looked once. Three times max.

When I reach the top of the stairs, Sophie yells, "Ta-dah!" Her stuffed animals are lined up on a faded red sofa. She grabs a bunny from the end and gives me way more detail than I need about how he got his name and her favorite things about him. She puts him back and picks up a yellow bear, then a red bear. My eyes start to cross from all the details on at least thirty stuffed animals. I don't have any experience with little girls. I'm the oldest of four boys, and Mom isn't the girly type. I have girl cousins, but when we were little, I ignored them in favor of playing with the boys.

I glance at May, who's covertly straightening up, putting Sophie's jacket away, throwing out tissues.

"No need to clean up for me," I say.

May laughs and holds her hands up. "Caught!"

She stands next to me, watching Sophie proudly introducing her stuffed animal family. My senses go on full alert, tuned into May. The need to touch the soft curve of her cheek makes my fingers twitch.

Nope. No touching. Unless she makes the first move.

May lets out an almost imperceptible sigh before saying, "Time out. We'll cover more stuffed animals on another day. Mason's a very busy man. He needs to look at the repair work now."

Sophie grabs a unicorn with a rainbow horn. "Then I'll just show you my favorite—Hornbow. He's on *Twinkle Fairies*. Do you like that show?"

"I don't know," I say. "I've never seen *Twinkle Fairies*."

May speaks in an authoritative voice. "Time to show Mason what needs to be fixed."

Sophie tucks Hornbow under her arm and grabs my hand. "Come on. I'll show you the dent I accidentally made in the wall."

I follow her downstairs with May trailing behind us.

Sophie talks a mile a minute about Hornbow's time at sharing day at her school and how all her friends wanted a turn to play with him.

"Popular unicorn," I say, stepping onto the second floor.

"I'm popular too," she says matter-of-factly.

Sophie skips ahead to a bedroom and pushes the door open. I step in with May and inspect the wall, where it looks like the doorknob smashed into it. I glance down at a doorstop installed in the baseboard.

"Someone threw open the door before the doorstop was installed?" I ask.

May looks meaningfully at Sophie, who protests, "I didn't throw the door. I just pushed it really fast."

"Next room," May says.

We continue our tour of the house. May shares her vision for the inn as we go. It's awesome to see the passion in her expressive face, her enthusiastic voice. Sophie gets bored and makes her way downstairs to watch TV in the family room.

After I finish cataloging the interior repairs, May leads me to the back windows in the family room, where Sophie looks hypnotized by her show and doesn't even notice us. May points out the deer-fence damage. It's a six-foot, wire-mesh deer fence. One of the posts is askew, and the fence is flattened low enough for other deer to get in. Apparently, a deer tried to jump the fence, fell on it, and scrambled over the dented fence. No problem.

"Oh, and the light fixtures are over here," May says.

I follow her to a corner with a collection of boxes for sconces, a couple of hanging lights, and a dining room chandelier. After she shows me where she wants everything, I've got a good idea of what to bring when I come back on New Year's Day.

She walks me to the door. "Thanks again, Mason. It'll be such a relief to finally be finished. I'm hoping to get the word out and open with a bang for Valentine's Day weekend."

"Valentine's Day and banging go perfectly together," I quip. *Inappropriate. Keep it clean.*

She puts a hand over her face, pink suffusing her cheeks. "I didn't mean it that way."

Sophie pops up by my side. "You're leaving already?"

"Yup. But I'll be back on New Year's Day to start fixing stuff."

"You can get a late start if you have plans for New Year's Eve," May says.

Sophie gets excited. "Come over for New Year's Eve! Mommy and I watch *Surprise Princess* parts one, two, and three and have sparkling water with potato chips."

I smile. "That sounds like a rocking night."

"I'm sure Mason has other plans," May says.

Sophie stares up at me with big puppy-dog eyes. "Do you?"

I clear my throat. "Yes, actually. I'm going to my cousin Owen's wedding."

Sophie grabs the end of her dress on both sides. "Ooh, I'd love to go to a wedding and dance." She twirls several times and stops suddenly. "I've never been to a wedding, but Olivia H. says you get cake and dance like crazy."

May puts a hand on Sophie's shoulder. "Weddings are planned well in advance. Mason can't add someone at the last minute. Besides, we don't want to miss our *Surprise Princess* marathon."

Sophie's shoulders droop, her expression falling. Happy to devastated in a flash.

"You can both go as my plus one," I say impulsively.

Sophie lights up, a big smile on her face. "Really?"

"You don't have a date?" May asks.

I shrug. "Some women get the wrong idea when you invite them to a wedding. You don't date, so we're good. Sophie's excited. What do you think?" I tense, suddenly really wanting May to go with me. And Sophie too. I like making her happy.

May's brows scrunch together as she thinks it over.

"Puh-leeze!" Sophie starts. I hold up a hand and shake my head. She instantly quiets.

"Owen won't mind," I assure May. "It's a ritzy affair, and believe me, they can afford it. It'll be here in town at Ludbury House."

May looks at Sophie, who clasps her hands together in prime begging fashion.

I continue, "Owen's marrying Shayla Adler. Have you seen her work? Movies, TV. Probably the best-known one is—"

"*Breakdown*," May finishes for me, eyes wide. "Your cousin's marrying Shayla Adler?"

"Yeah."

May nods once. "I'll think about it."

Sophie leaps in the air, arms up in a V of victory. "Yay! Thinking means yes."

"Thinking means thinking." May turns to me. "Can I let you know later today?"

My lips curve up. "Absolutely. Let me give you my number."

She pulls out her phone, does the code, and hands it over. I grin at the pink phone case. "You a fan of Hello Kitty?"

"My great-grandmom was, and she got me into it when I was a kid. I guess now I just like the reminder of her."

I hand back the phone. Her expression is a little sad.

"Grandmom Maggie was a badass!" Sophie exclaims.

"I told you we don't say the *b* word," May says. "It's not polite."

"Aunt Alice says it," Sophie says. "Is Aunt Alice rude?"

"It's a grown-up word," May says with a note of finality. She gives me an apologetic look.

"Great to see the place," I say. "See ya soon."

I let myself out. I'm halfway down the sidewalk when my phone chimes with a text from May: *Thanks for stopping by. Sorry if Sophie was in your face too much. I'll keep her busy when you're fixing stuff.*

No prob. In your face pretty much describes my entire family.
Ha!

I get into my truck and start it, turning the heat up. It's

freezing in here. I was at May's place longer than I thought. I send a quick text while the truck warms up. *Hope Sophie gets to eat cake and dance at the wedding.*

Three dots appear and then disappear.

Well, it was Sophie's idea. I just spontaneously asked them both. I exhale sharply and back out of the driveway.

I head towards home. No big. I'll go to the wedding solo like I was planning and do the usual, dance with someone pretty and not related to me. One of Shayla's friends should be fun.

I never should've asked May in the first place.

3
___

May

"He didn't want to go with me in the first place!" I whisper-shout to Alice. We're in the kitchen at her place. Sophie's doing a tiger jigsaw puzzle Alice keeps for her in the living room.

Alice levels me with a determined look and lifts a finger. "One, he's doing free repairs for you on his time off." Another finger goes up. "Two, men don't ask you to a wedding if they don't mean it."

"He only said that because Sophie was excited by the idea of a wedding."

She holds up another finger. "Three, he's hot."

I groan. "Alice."

"It's a fact. Why do you think the ratings are so high on his show? He's gorgeous. That's the real reason you watch, isn't it?"

I take a sip of tea. "I like learning about cars."

"Bullshit."

"Shh. Sophie's right there. Did I tell you she said badass in front of him?"

Alice giggles. "Oops. That was from me."

"No kidding."

"Did she call him a badass?"

"She was talking about Grandmom Maggie."

Alice gets serious. "There's your answer. WWMD?" She means What Would Maggie Do? We often think of her when we need a little extra courage to do something. She always colored outside the lines. The woman wore a leopard body-suit with a tutu in her nineties. She seduced her much younger tango instructor. She said exactly what she thought, and she did as she pleased, even if that meant eating Snickers for breakfast, stealing Dad's Harley, or ziplining. All that was in her seventies! God, I miss her.

I look to the ceiling. "WWMD doesn't apply here."

"Sure it does."

"Grandmom was never a single mom."

"But you and Sophie can both go. Come on, it'll be fun. You can dance, mingle with a few movie stars, and tell me every detail. I'd go in a heartbeat."

I smile. "You can go for me and take Sophie. It's perfect."

"I haven't pretended to be you since high school. We're grownups now. Besides, Sophie would give it away."

I frown. She's right. I don't know why I'm so worked up over going to a wedding. It's not a date. There'll be lots of other people there besides Mason. I'll probably spend most of the time keeping Sophie out of trouble.

I dig my heels in. "I'm not ready to date. I plan to wait until Sophie's in college."

Alice smiles slyly. "I thought you said it wasn't a date. Just friends."

"Right."

"So there should be no problem."

I glance over at Sophie. She finished the puzzle and is curled up on the sofa, reading a chapter book under a blanket knitted by Grandmom Maggie. WWMD? Something *wild*.

Alice takes my hand. "Please let yourself have a little fun. You deserve it."

Suddenly I know just how to color outside the lines. I lean across the table. "Here's what we'll do."

Alice groans. "There should *not* be a we in there."

I grin. "Come on, it'll be fun. You said yourself you're getting bored with Charlie being away for New Year's." Alice's husband, Charlie, went skiing with some old high school friends over New Year's. Alice gave her blessing. She doesn't like skiing. They're happily married, no kids by choice. They travel often, enjoying their freedom. And, of course, Sophie gives them a kid fix whenever they want.

"I'm not *that* bored," Alice says.

I warm to my idea. "Just listen. We'll both dress up like we're going to the wedding, and when he comes to the door, if he picks the right twin, then I'll go."

"And what if he picks me?"

"Then you get to have a great time dancing and mingling with movie stars. It's perfect."

Alice sighs. "I know you're scared—"

"I'm not scared of anything. This'll be *wild*. Grandmom always thought it was a hoot when we switched places."

"Only because she always knew who was who."

I give her my best pleading look.

"Fine. But I still think—"

I leap out of my seat and hug her. "Thank you."

She pulls back. "You owe me."

"Anything."

"I'll hold you to that."

My pulse accelerates at the idea of Mason choosing me. I could be going to a wedding with a complete hottie. And if not, I'll know he's not that into me, proving Alice wrong.

Mason

I wave to Sophie staring at me through the front window as I approach their house on New Year's Eve. She grins, waving back, then disappears from view. I was surprised when May texted me they'd go to the wedding. In a good way. I'm still unsure how to deal with a little girl, but I figure I'll take my cue from May. She's the mom, and it's not like I'm ready to be a dad. That's for future Mason. Way, way in the future.

I blow out a breath, suddenly nervous. Like I'm a teenager on a first date. Ridiculous. I've been on plenty of dates, plenty of relationships that went nowhere. Doesn't matter. This is a friend situation.

I ring the bell, and the door opens a moment later.

Sophie stands there in a red velvet dress, white tights, and shiny black shoes. "This is my Christmas dress."

"Cool."

I step inside and shut the door behind me. "Could you get your mom for me?"

"Mommy!" she yells at the top of her lungs.

"I could've done that."

Her nose crinkles. "She's not your mommy."

"I know. I..." I trail off as two beautiful women appear, wearing identical black dresses, their hair up in a twist, silver earrings dangling from their ears.

It's a test. The identical twin switcheroo. May wants to know that I see her for her. Truth is, dressed the same, hair the same, they truly are identical.

I turn to the woman on the left, studying her closely. "You look beautiful."

"Thank you."

Then I turn to the woman on the right. "As does my plus one."

May's lips part in surprise. She blinks a few times. Ha! I passed.

Sophie giggles madly and claps. "He picked you, Mommy! Now you can go to the wedding."

Alice gives me an apologetic smile. "Sorry, just a little joke. It wasn't my idea."

"May should've known I couldn't be fooled." I shake my head at May. "I told you I have identical twin brothers and uncles who love to pull a switcheroo."

She nods, blushing, and gets her and Sophie's coats from the closet. Alice helps Sophie with her coat, and I help May into hers.

She turns to face me. "How did you know?"

"It's the spark in your eyes. Also, Alice has a small scar on her chin."

She stares at me, clearly still in shock. Was she hoping I'd pick Alice?

I search her expression. "And I noticed that your skin is flawless."

She sucks in air.

"Nice," Alice says with a big smile.

I offer my arm to May, and she takes it. As soon as I open the door, Sophie dashes through it.

"Walk!" May yells. "There's still ice."

Sophie walks at a pace that's nearly a run. She's excited.

A few moments later, I open the back door of my freshly washed truck and help Sophie in.

She does her seatbelt on her own. Spying the wrapped wedding gift on the seat next to her, she grabs it. "Is this for me?"

"No. It's a wedding gift."

Her face falls. "Oh." She puts it back on the seat. Now I wish I'd gotten her a present. Just something small, like a corsage. Damn, I should've gotten them both corsages. I shut her door.

May's already opened the passenger door. I shift so I can close it behind her.

She goes to get in and stops, turning and bringing us eye to eye. She's close enough I can see the gold flecks in her hazel eyes. "I still can't believe you could tell me and Alice apart so easily."

"The chemistry only works with one of you."

Her cheeks flush, and she gets into the truck. Damn. I probably shouldn't have admitted that inconvenient truth.

I shut the door and make my way to the driver's seat. Maybe she wasn't hoping I'd pick Alice. Maybe she tested me because she's into me. If she wasn't, she wouldn't care if I could pick her out. She wants to be special in my eyes.

May

I study Mason's profile as he pulls out onto the street. Square jaw, those thick lashes, his sensual lips. I don't usually notice details about a man. In fact, I don't meet a lot of men besides repairmen. Well, there was my ex last year from work. I guess it's been a while since I've spent time with a man as friends.

I still can't believe Mason passed the twin test. No one passes it that early on, not even family. Only my parents and great-grandmother Maggie always knew who was who. Mom says when we were babies, they dressed me in pink and Alice in purple so they wouldn't get confused. Once our personalities became clear, they didn't have to stick to a color scheme. My sister's adventurous, and I'm cautious. But what has that gotten me in life? I followed a plan—college, marriage, a baby—and the plan blew up in my face. Rick died. Working and raising Sophie by myself is a million times harder than when I had Rick to help. He was a hands-on dad.

"So I thought I'd give you a quick rundown of the family," Mason says. "I'll start with my uncle Jake since he ties most closely to the bridal couple. He's Owen's dad. The bride, Shayla, is close with Uncle Jake's wife, Claire. She took Shayla in when Shayla was a teen actor going off the rails. That's how Owen and Shayla met the first time."

"Is your aunt Claire an actor too?" I ask. "Is that how she knows Shayla?"

"Yup. Claire Jordan."

My jaw drops. Everyone knows Claire Jordan. She's a *huge* movie star.

"She's more behind-the-scenes now as a director and producer, but you'll still see her acting in a few projects."

Double the star power at this wedding. Now I'm wondering if we can fit in with this crowd. I glance back at Sophie, who's all ears, silently taking it in.

Mason continues, "Uncle Jake is the one with the identical twin, Uncle Josh. Josh owns Happy Endings bar."

My brain fires off connections. I know Josh and his family. If he has an identical twin, they're probably close, which means I could've met Mason's family at any time. And that means meeting Mason was inevitable. Like fate. Or just six degrees of separation from Uncle Josh.

"Am I going too fast?" Mason asks, glancing at me.

"I can't believe we haven't met before. I already know some of your family."

"Yeah, we're at Happy Endings regularly, celebrating one family event or another."

"I haven't been in a while since I've been so busy with the house and life stuff."

"You're practically one of us already. Just wait until Josh hears about your twin test. He'll love it."

"I definitely need to hear his story."

"I'll let Uncle Josh tell it."

"I want a twin too!" Sophie chirps.

"Too late. You have to be born with one," Mason says. "I used to wish that too. But you know what? It's cool to be just you."

"Then I want a little sister," Sophie says. "I can dress her up and push her in a stroller."

I close my eyes. First she wants a daddy and then a sister.

I turn to face her. "You can do the same with Sissy." That's her baby doll.

"Sissy isn't the same as a real live girl," Sophie says.

"We're here," Mason announces, parking in the back lot behind Ludbury House.

Thank God. I'm not up to reasoning with Sophie on why our family's already complete. She doesn't buy it now that she knows her friends have dads and siblings. I need to finesse a *there's all kinds of families* speech.

As soon as Mason turns off the truck, Sophie clambers out the door. I hurry out of the truck. "Freeze!"

Sophie freezes.

"Now walk back to me."

I put a hand on her shoulder. "Stay with us."

"Hey, Sophie," Mason says as he opens the back door of the truck. "Do you want to carry the wedding present in?"

Her eyes get big, and she runs over to him, holding out her hands. He sets a small rectangular box in her hands with a card attached.

She shakes it.

He steadies the box. "Careful. It's fragile."

"What is it?" she asks.

"A framed picture of Shayla and Owen with a bunch of us cousins when we were teenagers."

"You were a teenager?" Sophie asks.

"I was a baby once too," he says.

Sophie cracks up at this. Guess she can't imagine the man ever being a baby.

Mason offers his arm, so I take it. Heat rushes through my body. I make a point of looking at Ludbury House and not him as we approach. I've passed this place so many times, but never had an invite to a private event held here. It's a sprawling two-and-a-half-story white clapboard mansion with white columns and a wraparound porch. I'm starting to feel like I'm Cinderella for the night.

Mason

Ludbury House is decorated with a winter white theme with silver and white silk streamers and plenty of white flowers. My aunt Hailey approaches. She's wearing a headset over her long strawberry blonde hair with a blue dress and heels. She's working. It belatedly occurs to me I should've told Hailey, the wedding planner, that I was bringing two guests. I cleared it with Shayla and Owen. I'm not sure if they passed the message along.

"Hi, Mason." She kisses my cheek. "I see you brought a

plus two." She smiles at them. "Hi, May, hi, Sophie." She glances at me. "We've met at Happy Endings before."

"Hello," May says.

"Hi!" Sophie says. "I brought the present." She hands it to Hailey.

"Thank you. I'll put this on the gift table. Let me just rustle up a couple more chairs, and we can welcome you into the parlor."

She hurries off, her heels clicking on the hardwood floor.

May grabs my arm, and it warms on the spot. "They're not expecting us?"

"I cleared it with the bride and groom, but I guess they forgot to pass it on to Aunt Hailey. It's no problem. She runs weddings at Ludbury House like clockwork. Nothing throws her."

May puts a hand over her face, embarrassed. Sophie takes that opportunity to rush into the parlor. May drops her hand, realizes Sophie's gone, and looks panicked.

"She went into the parlor." I gesture to the room on our right.

We arrive in the room to find Sophie standing in front of the fireplace. She touches each white flower draped across the mantel and sniffs them. Rows of folding chairs draped in white fill the space. There're probably around fifty guests. Looks like Sophie's the only kid. Hope she behaves herself. Flower sniffing seems okay to me.

May rushes to Sophie, takes her by the hand, and guides her to the back of the room.

"Let's sit down," Sophie says. "There's lots of empty chairs."

"Those seats are taken," May says. She turns to me. "I feel bad that Hailey has to do last minute extra work to accommodate us."

"I'll go help her. The chairs are stored in the basement." I used to play here with my cousins sometimes.

I go down to the basement. Hailey's voice carries as she confirms the bride has everything she needs in the bridal suite. As I step closer, I see she's talking to Rowan, my cousin Cooper's fiancée. She always has a serious expression except when she's with Cooper. Rowan works with Hailey at her wedding planning business, Love Junkies.

"Hey, I came down to carry some chairs," I say.

"Great!" Hailey points to them. "Rowan, can you get extra white slipcovers from my office so they match?"

"On it." Rowan hurries upstairs.

I pick up the chairs. "Sorry for the unexpected guests. Shayla and Owen okayed it."

Hailey steps closer. "I didn't know you were dating a single mom."

"Just a friend thing. I'm doing some repairs on her place over on Catoonah. It's going to be an inn soon."

"Oh, I know all about that place. It's across the street from Mackenzie and Harper. May's nice."

"Yeah, she is." My voice comes out husky. "See you later."

I head upstairs.

"You look natural together," Hailey calls after me. "Sometimes you find someone you can relax around, and that can be a perfect fit."

"No matchmaking," I throw over my shoulder. Aunt Hailey has a well-earned reputation for being a matchmaker. According to her, she helped all of her friends find love. Now she's working on the second generation, all the kids of her friends. My cousins and I like to find our own dates, thank you very much.

I set the chairs on either side of the back row. People can still get by them if they need to. Rowan puts on the white slipcovers and leaves.

Sophie sits happily on the end seat. "Mason, sit next to me."

May stiffens. I gesture for May to go into the row.

She takes the seat next to Sophie, who says, "Leave room in the middle for Mason."

May sighs and scoots over one.

"You're very popular," she says to me after I take my seat.

"I know."

"Where's the cake?" Sophie asks me.

"In the ballroom. We'll have cake when it's time at the reception."

"What's a reception?"

"It's the party after."

"Oh." She grins and kicks her legs. "Awesome."

My parents walk in and stare at me sitting next to two strangers. Mom recovers first. "Mason, did you bring guests?" Mom has a short bob of brown hair that emphasizes her sharp features, especially those all-knowing eyes.

"Yes, this is May and her daughter, Sophie. They're my plus two."

"Hi," Mom says, looking from me to Sophie and back to May.

"Nice to meet you," Dad says, always the more easygoing one.

Sophie stares at my dad, her eyes wide. "Parker! Can I get your autograph too?"

Dad grins. "You like *Hot Finds*?"

"We watch it every week," May says.

Sophie nods vigorously.

Dad points to her. "I'll catch up with you at the reception for that autograph."

My parents sit several rows up next to my uncle Josh and an empty chair that will be for my aunt Hailey. Mom whispers fiercely to her older brother, Josh, who takes a peek back at us.

I lift a hand in greeting.

He jerks his chin and turns back.

May leans close to whisper, "Mason, you didn't tell me it was a small wedding. Is everyone here family?"

"Some friends too."

"Sophie and I stick out like a sore thumb."

"You must recognize some people. There's definitely some Clover Park residents here."

She looks around. "I know Josh, Hailey, and their kids."

"See?"

We wait as more people come filing in. There's a low whisper moving through the room, and several of my relatives turn around to look at us. Just because I've never brought a woman and her daughter to a wedding is no cause for gossip.

I glare at every single one of them. May already feels awkward joining a small family wedding. I don't want to make it any worse. I want her to have a good time.

"Will you dance with me?" Sophie asks me.

How can I say no? "Sure, and your mom too."

"Everyone will dance together," May says with a note of finality.

Aunt Hailey takes her seat, talks to Uncle Josh, and turns around to wave at us.

I give a quick wave. May looks uncomfortable.

"You okay?" I whisper to May.

"Fine."

"Really?"

"Well, other than the fact that your entire family keeps turning around to look at me, and I'm crashing the small family wedding of a famous actor, everything's great." She catches my brothers looking at her. "Why does everyone keep looking at me?"

"Probably because I never invite women to a wedding. I made an exception because I wanted you both to experience cake and dancing. Right, Sophie?"

"Right!"

I give May's hand a squeeze to reassure her. She stares at my hand on hers and pulls away, shifting in her seat. *Ouch.*

Clearly she doesn't like my touch. Even for a friendly gesture. I'll keep my distance. After today, I'll only see her at her home, where I'll be busy doing repairs.

No problem.

She glances at me with a tight smile and faces front. A tension simmers between us and not the good kind.

The processional music starts up, and the bridal party

makes their way down the short aisle. Things have to get better at the reception. Right?

4

———

The ceremony was beautiful. Shayla and Owen both choked up saying their vows. They fell in love at sixteen just like me and Rick. At our wedding, there were no tears or choked voices throughout the vows, only beaming smiles. We both felt like it was destiny after being high school sweethearts and dating for so many years. No wonder I'm afraid to love again. Love at such a tender age is precious. It feels wrong to even imagine my life with anyone else.

Now we're in the ballroom for the wedding reception. The moment the music starts, Sophie dashes onto the dance floor. I'm half embarrassed, half proud of the way she dances like no one's watching when *everyone* is. She's the only one out there.

Mason is talking to one of his cousins by the bar. Should I join her out there? I'm not keen on being the center of attention, but she's my daughter. Sophie often requires me to step out of my comfort zone. I've been called in for little "chats" with her preschool teacher last year way too often. Sophie has her own agenda and sees no issue with following it. One day this will be useful to her in life.

A brunette woman around my age in a red dress raises her arms and says to Sophie, "Girl, shake it." She joins Sophie on the dance floor, and they dance together. The woman takes Sophie's hand and twirls her around. Sophie's thrilled.

Mason joins me. "That's my cousin Viv with Sophie. She loves kids. She's a teacher at a Montessori school."

I relax. Seems like a good person for Sophie to be around. "Sophie's having a blast."

"Do you want to join them?"

"Oh, no. I'll wait until there's more people on the dance floor. Dancing and cake were Sophie's priority."

He gives me a sexy half smile that makes my heart beat faster. "What's yours?"

I watch Sophie. "Well, I guess to have fun and meet more locals now that we're living here permanently. A lot of the people I knew growing up have moved away."

"Sure. Networking for the inn."

"I didn't mean it like that. Just, you know, expanding my social circle. My family's here, so I'm not lonely or anything." *Except for the long nights alone with my worries over Sophie, the future, and my career.*

He tilts his head, studying me.

"Enough about me." I glance at the dance floor. The bride and groom, Shayla and Owen, joined Sophie and Viv. "Shayla's a radiant bride, isn't she?"

"Yeah. They're happy. They got together as teens, fell hard for each other, and then broke up. They both had a lot of growing up to do. And then when Shayla came back to town for an acting gig, they reunited."

"Sounds like a fairy tale."

He laughs. "Not as simple as that. They had their ups and downs before finally giving in to the inevitable. I always knew by the way Owen refused to talk about her or watch any of her movies or TV shows that he was still stuck on her."

"She's certainly beautiful, and she seemed nice when you introduced us."

"Her inside matches the outside." He jerks his chin at someone. "Come on, I'll introduce you around."

"Okay, but don't mention the Serenity Inn. I don't want it to seem like I'm scouting for business."

"It might come up. They'll want to know how we know each other."

"Just say we ran into each other at Happy Endings."

He's quiet for a moment. "All right. We'll do it your way."

"Why did you hesitate?"

"Because saying we met at a bar sends a different message than I'm doing repairs at the inn."

He's right. It sounds like he picked me up at a bar or vice versa. Not so much a friend thing.

He leans close. "Incoming. Don't worry."

The parents of the groom approach. Oh my God, I can't believe I'm meeting Claire Jordan. She looks effortlessly glamourous with her blond hair up in a twist and her shimmery lavender dress. Her husband, Jake Campbell, looks like a more sophisticated version of his identical twin, Josh. His dark brown hair is cut short; his navy suit custom made to his frame.

Mason gives his uncle a bro hug and kisses his aunt on the cheek. "Uncle Jake, Aunt Claire, this is May."

Jake reaches out to shake my hand. "Nice to meet you, May."

I shake his hand. "You too."

Claire smiles at me. "Very nice to meet you. You two look good together."

I gesture back and forth between me and Mason. "Oh, we're not a couple. We just met. He's fixing stuff for me at the house."

"We're friends," Mason says firmly.

Claire raises a skeptical brow.

I clamp my mouth shut so I don't overexplain the friend thing. I kinda want her autograph. She's older than me, I'd guess late forties or fifties, but the image I remember best from her most famous movies is when she's closer to my age. That's how I'll forever think of her.

I realize I'm lost in thought, staring at Claire, when I

nearly jump out of my skin as little hands grab my leg. I let out a breath and put a hand on Sophie's hair, smoothing it out of her flushed face. "Are you having fun out there?"

"Yes. When's the cake?"

"They'll announce when it's time. Sophie, this is Mason's uncle Jake and aunt Claire."

"Hi," she says, barely looking at them. She doesn't notice it's Claire Jordan, but she recognized Mason right away? Kids.

A slow song starts. Jake looks to Claire in question. I make sure not to look at Mason.

Sophie grabs Mason's hand and pulls. "You said you'd dance with me."

"Is it okay with you?" he asks me.

"Sure."

I watch as Sophie drags him out to the dance floor.

"Maybe you can cut in on them," Claire says to me. She winks and walks off to dance with her husband.

Mason takes Sophie's hands and tells her something. She steps onto his feet, and he starts dancing, moving her in slow circles.

She looks up at him and beams. My heart skips a beat. *Don't get attached.* I'm not sure if I'm more worried about her or myself.

Within moments, the dance floor is packed with couples, most of them gazing lovingly into each other's eyes. That's nice. Reminds me of my family. My parents and my aunts and uncles all have long, happy marriages. I always thought I'd have the same with Rick.

Hailey joins me. "Hello!"

"Beautiful wedding," I say. "You really know your stuff. I've never been to a winter wedding."

"Thank you. I've done all kinds. Once I even did a Halloween-themed wedding."

"That must've been interesting."

She gestures animatedly. "It was so cool. We had cobwebs, skull lights, jack o'lanterns. The bride wore black, of course.

The groom had a cape and fangs. Anyway, I haven't seen you out on the dance floor. Why don't you join me on the next fast song?"

I flush with embarrassment. "Sure." She feels bad for me, being a stranger to most of these people. I didn't think it would be such a small wedding, where Sophie and I are points of interest.

Hailey smiles widely. "Mason's a good one. He had a serious relationship once, so he's capable of it. Just needs to find the right woman."

I stare straight ahead. "Mmm, I hope he finds her."

Finally, the slow song ends. Sophie dances madly to the next song with a thumping bass beat, and Mason walks off, looking for someone. Our gazes collide, and he heads toward me. I find myself smiling.

"Mason, join us on the dance floor," Hailey says.

"Actually, I have to do a small secret errand for the bride and groom. I'll be back before you know it." He turns to me. "You okay with that?"

"Of course. No problem."

He smiles and then jogs from the ballroom.

Hailey squeezes my shoulder. "Don't worry, he'll be back."

"Oh, I'm not worried."

"Good, let's dance."

After our fast dance, I excuse myself to get some water from the pitcher at the table. I feel strange dancing with Mason's curious family, who seem to be studying me while they smile. Is Sophie the only reason he invited us? I don't know why else his family would find *me* so interesting.

I set the glass down and decide to step out to the ladies' room for a bit of quiet. Sophie's in the middle of things, dancing up a storm. She probably won't notice I'm gone.

Mason meets me just as I step into the hallway. "Hi. Sorry

to leave you alone. We went out to decorate the car for the bride and groom. We had to keep it discreet since Shayla needs security, so it was mostly on the inside of the car."

"What'd you put in there?"

"A small banner saying congratulations on one window and a liberal pile of rainbow condoms and edible underwear."

My jaw drops. "Seriously?"

He grins. "It was Nathan's idea. He's Owen's closest friend and business partner. I'm sure there'll be retaliation if Nathan ever gets married. Come on, I'll introduce you to some more people."

So much for a peaceful refuge in the ladies' room, though I have to admit I feel much more comfortable when Mason's with me. But then he leads me toward his parents.

"I met them briefly earlier," I say, a little concerned about why Mason wants his parents to get to know me.

"They want to talk to you."

I approach them with a pleasant expression, even though I'm nervous. I don't need to get their approval since Mason is just a friend. I wipe my clammy hands on the sides of my dress.

"Hi," I say.

His dad, Parker, smiles. His mom says, "Hey."

I feel like I know his dad, Parker, from TV. He's a chill guy and an expert mechanic. His mom, with her short bob of brown hair and sharp brown eyes, looks tough, like she takes no BS from anyone. I wouldn't want to cross her.

"May's opening the inn across the street from Mackenzie and Harper's place," Mason tells them.

Parker gives me a sweet smile that reminds me of Mason's. "I heard about the inn. How's it going?"

"Almost ready." I cross my fingers. "Hoping for a full inn when I open on Valentine's Day weekend."

His mom and dad nod.

Mason smiles. "You'll get there."

His mom studies me for a moment before saying, "How old is your daughter?"

"Sophie's five. She started kindergarten this year." I glance over to the dance floor, where Sophie's twirling this way and that, trying to get her dress to puff out. She's having the time of her life. The things I do for her. The level of awkwardness for me tonight has reached all new levels.

Mason takes my hand. "Come on, let's dance." He pulls me away from his parents. I say a quick bye to them, so relieved to step away that I don't even worry about dancing with him. He leads us to the far corner of the dance floor, away from their curious eyes.

"You definitely take after your dad," I say.

He smiles, his brown eyes dancing with amusement. "True. Mom's a little rough around the edges. I'm told she mellowed with age. Have you ever met a blackbelt, fearless woman who kicks ass and takes names?"

"I have now."

He starts moving to the beat. He has good rhythm. *Don't think about what that means.*

I start dancing, hoping his parents aren't watching us. "Your mom must've been strict."

"Not at all, but she had certain rules, mostly meant to keep us boys from killing each other. Things got physical between me and my brothers in a heartbeat. Mom put a laminated poster in the kitchen to remind us how to settle arguments, the order of who sits in the front seat of the car, and who gets the TV remote on what day. That kind of thing."

"Wow. My sister and I were peaceful and played together nicely."

"You never fought?"

"We argued, especially as teens, but it never got physical."

I'm not sure who moves first, but we're suddenly closer, dancing in time to the thumping beat. My world narrows down to him. His gaze shifts from my eyes to my cheek to my lips. I lick them, suddenly self-conscious. I can feel the heat of his body, and I'm hyperaware of mine, every nerve standing at attention.

The song ends suddenly, and I pull away, overwhelmed by the intensity. I glance at him. He looks as dazed as I feel. Another song picks up with a line dance. That seems much safer.

We join in. It's a relief to stand next to him but not so close. He smiles at me when he misses a step and gamely corrects course.

A series of fun dances follows—the chicken dance, the hokey-pokey, and finally, "Twist and Shout."

I'm flushed with exertion, enjoying myself more than I thought I would. "Twist and Shout" ends, and a slow song starts. I freeze, part of me wanting to slow dance with Mason, part of me terrified of feeling too much for a man I need to keep in the friend zone.

Sophie runs over to Mason. Her hair's damp with sweat, her color high. "Let's dance again." She grabs his arms and steps on his feet.

Mason lifts her off his feet. "Actually, I'm going to dance with your mom." My heart lurches. This is dangerous territory.

She brushes the hair from her face. "Okay. I'm sweaty."

"I'll get you some water," I say, taking her hand and walking off the dance floor.

After I pour her a glass of water from a pitcher on our table, my eye catches on Mason. He's across the room, his eyes locked on me. A shiver runs down my spine. There's something between us, an attraction. I need to keep my distance.

After the slow song, the music picks up with "YMCA," and we all crowd the dance floor. Mason shows Sophie the moves. His cousins Mackenzie and Harper join us. They're my neighbors across the street. Both have long brown hair, Harper's a shade lighter. They could pass for sisters even though they're cousins.

I laugh, watching everyone do the letters to the song.

Mackenzie really bends her body to look like the YMCA letters.

Harper hitches a thumb at her. "Former cheerleader."

Mackenzie smiles brightly. "And I work out to keep up my flexibility."

When the song ends, Mason says, "Excuse me, looks like my dad needs me."

I walk off the dance floor with Mackenzie and Harper. "That was fun."

"It was," Mackenzie says. "Mason's into you. I can tell."

I try valiantly not to blush and fail. "Just friends," I mutter. Who knew his family would be so eager to put us together? I'm sure he meets plenty of women.

Mackenzie turns me slightly and gestures with her elbow at the best man, Nathan, a man with dark hair and piercing blue eyes. "See the way Nathan's looking at Harper?"

I nod. His gaze can only be described as longing.

"He is not," Harper says, checking for herself and turning back to us. "It was a coincidence. He looked over here because we looked over."

Mackenzie continues, "That moon-eyed look that Nathan gave to Harper, that's the way Mason looks at you."

Harper crosses her arms. "A guy can look at someone without it meaning anything. May, I get it. You and Mason are just friends, like me and Nathan are longtime acquaintances."

Mackenzie laughs. "Come on. You—"

Harper huddles in close. "He's coming over here."

A slow song starts.

Harper looks for escape. "Shit, shit, shit. Let's go to the ladies' room and freshen up." Before she can pull Mackenzie away, Nathan's arrived. The man could be a model.

He flashes a smile. "Hello, ladies. Harper."

She glares at him.

"That's better than your dead-to-me stare," he says. "Dance with me."

Harper lifts her chin. "Is that an order?"

"Please."

Mackenzie pushes her. "Go ahead; dance with your long-time acquaintance."

Harper sighs. "Fine. I'll dance with you."

They walk to the dance floor with Harper in the lead. Mackenzie points to the bar. "That's our cue. Want to get a drink?"

"Sure."

We walk toward the bar. "It's a miracle she's dancing with him," Mackenzie says. "After we get our drinks, I've got to get a picture."

"What's their deal?"

"They were best friends when we were little. He's a neighbor of hers, so they grew up together. Something happened at prom that made her despise him. I have no idea what. I'm guessing she made a move, and he rejected her."

"Life's too short to hold a grudge," I say.

"Right? Though when it comes to the heart, I get it. I still want my ex to burn in hell." We reach the bar. "Champagne?"

"Sure."

We get our drinks and head toward the side of the room. I catch Mason's eye. His dad looks serious, talking to him. Mason looks away, frowning. Hope it's not bad news.

Mackenzie leads us to a table by the edge of the dance floor.

"Oh, the picture," Mackenzie says, putting her drink down. "Where are they?"

I point toward the left, where Nathan and Harper are now standing still in dance position, having a heated exchange of angry words.

"Oh no," Mackenzie mutters.

Harper jerks away and stalks off the dance floor, heading toward the bar. Nathan goes after her. She stops dead in her tracks, turns and says something that makes him back off with his palms in the air.

Nathan shoots Mackenzie a wry look and shrugs. She turns to me. "I swear he's a good guy. We're partners in a tech security business with Owen."

"They say love and hate aren't that far apart."

"My parents are proof," she says with a laugh. "Frenemies 'til the inevitable end."

"How's that?" I ask.

Mason joins us. "Hey, they're cutting the cake now."

"Story for another day," Mackenzie says with a smile.

I glance over at her parents standing close, Josh's arm around Hailey's shoulders, looking perfectly content. Hard to picture them as frenemies.

Sophie comes bouncing along. "Finally, cake!"

We gather around to watch them cut the cake. I catch Mason looking at me, and he quickly turns away, glancing at his dad and looking guilty.

What's that about?

∾

Mason

I'm quiet on the short drive back to May's place. Sophie's asleep in the back seat after wearing herself out dancing. I had a great time with May. She's fun and sweet. I'm not used to sweet, and I really like it. Until Dad pulled me aside for a talk. I can count on one hand the number of times he's had a serious talk with me. He's always been more of a *life is the best teacher* kind of guy.

His warning runs through my head. "Tread carefully with a single mom. Don't lead her on. A young girl like Sophie is very impressionable. If things don't work out, you'll be hurting both of them."

I assured him we were just friends and it was no problem. He clearly didn't buy it. I guess he could tell I was having more fun dancing and talking to May than I have in a long while. It just feels good to be around her.

I look in the rearview mirror at a sleeping Sophie. The last thing I'd ever want is to hurt an innocent child, even if only by association through her mom. Sophie longs for a dad. If

I'm not ready to commit to that kind of life, which I'm not, then Dad's right, I shouldn't lead May on.

"Is everything okay?" May asks. "You're quiet."

"Just tired. Great wedding, though."

"Thanks for inviting us."

"Sure. Guess Sophie's not going to make it to midnight to toast with sparkling water."

May laughs, the sound warming me. "We celebrate New Year's Eve at nine p.m. at our house. Anyway, I think the whole night was a celebration for her."

"I'm glad she had fun." I clamp my mouth shut to keep the words back that I really want to say—I had an awesome time, and it was all because of you.

Keeping my distance is for the best.

When we arrive at her house a short time later, I turn to her. "Do you need help carrying Sophie in?"

"I got it."

She gets out of the truck and goes to get Sophie, who wakes up. I should at least walk them to the door. I get out and join them on the front walk. May walks with her arm around Sophie, who's stumbling along sleepily.

May unlocks the door and pushes it open. "Brush your teeth and go straight to bed."

Sophie walks inside like a zombie. "Too tired to brush my teeth." She heads upstairs.

May turns to me. "Good night and happy New Year." She lifts her arms like she wants to hug me and then switches to offering her hand.

I clasp her hand. An awkward goodbye. Our eyes meet, and I feel that same electric current that sizzled between us when we danced. Chemistry.

Her cheeks pinken. "Bye."

I take a step back. "I'm not sure if we can be friends." *Because I'm way too attracted to you.*

"Oh. I thought we both had a good time tonight."

I blow out a breath. "We did. It's just, you know, different with the single-mom thing."

"Ah, okay."

"Sophie's young—"

She holds up a palm. "No need to explain. In fact, I was thinking the same thing. Are you still going to be my handyman?"

"Yes," I say with some relief. It's not like this is goodbye forever. "I'll see you tomorrow."

"Okay. Bye, Mason."

Did her voice sound a little sad? Should I say it's not her just the situation?

I gesture toward her, struggling for the right words.

"Yes?"

I scratch my head, unsure why I'm lingering. "Bye." I turn and head out the door. Best not to drag things out. Rip the Band-Aid off and be done with it.

As I drive home, flashes of the night come back to me. The joy in May's face when we danced, her sweet smile, her laugh.

Sometimes doing the right thing feels so wrong.

5

The next day I show up at May's place with my supplies and toolbox. I expect it to be awkward now that I've announced we're not going to be friends. The best thing to do is treat this like a job. In and out. No need to talk to May beyond the scope of the work. I'll treat her just like I treat my clients, but with less smiling. I don't want to give her any mixed messages, especially while I'm pretending not to be attracted.

I head up the front walk. There's a snowman in the yard with a mop for hair, a carrot nose, and rocks for eyes and a melting mouth. I smile, remembering my brothers and me playing in the snow. We built forts and piles of snowballs for ammunition, pelting each other like we were at war. Michael's nose got broken by a well-timed frosty snowball from someone who might've been mad at him for snow down the collar. Good times.

Like most of our wild fun, that led to another Shaw family rule: no snowballs in the face. Those family rules grew as we did. Mom forced us to recite them together when any rule was broken. Sophie's lucky she doesn't have to worry about siblings and family rules.

But where would I be without my brothers? Sophie has no dad *and* no siblings. It must be kind of lonely. Not my concern. I'm here to help a friend. Well, not a friend. Just someone I met recently and went to a wedding with and that's all.

I ring the bell.

May answers the door with a bright smile. "Good morning." She's wearing a green baggy sweater over leggings, and all I can think about are the curves I know are hiding underneath.

"Morning." My voice sounds hoarse. *Chill.* I step inside.

Sophie appears wearing a big floppy hat and a swimsuit with a towel around her shoulders. Pink winter boots complete the outfit. She has a beach ball under one arm.

"It's beach day at our house," she says before throwing the beach ball at my head. It hits me, too, because I can't deflect when my hands are holding all this stuff.

"Sophie!" May exclaims. "Say you're sorry." She turns to me. "I'm so sorry. She's never done that before."

I put down my toolbox and supplies and pick up the beach ball. "I'm fine. My brothers and I did much worse to each other."

Sophie grabs the ball from my hands. "Like what?"

"Sophie, apologize," May says. "That was rude, especially to someone who's here on his vacation time to help us with the inn."

Sophie looks at my feet. "Sorry," she mumbles.

"You're forgiven."

She lifts her head and grins. "Have you ever been in a pool with a slide? I went once at Brittany's birthday party."

"Sure have."

May sighs. "Sophie, go put something warmer over that outfit. It's the middle of winter. Mason, would you like some coffee before you start? I could use some too."

I consider the invitation, the two of us sitting at her kitchen table. Too close.

"No, thanks." I gesture toward the stairs. "I'll get started in the second bedroom."

"Thank you. I'll keep Sophie out of your way."

"I have a big family. I'm used to focusing in chaos. Not

that Sophie's chaos. I'm sure she's very manageable or whatever the parent term is for kids being kept in line."

Her hazel eyes dance with amusement. "Parenting."

"Right." I head toward the stairs, embarrassed. I don't have to worry about keeping my distance. I do it without even trying by saying the wrong thing. You don't manage kids, you parent them. It's not a corporation.

I get to work, focused intently on repairing drywall. Loud thumps come from the ceiling above like Sophie's jumping on all the furniture or dancing. Is May with her? What do a mom and daughter do all day when there's no school? At our house growing up, I had built-in friends with my brothers. May must have to be like Sophie's friend sometimes.

Stop thinking about May and her life with Sophie.

I hear May talking to someone, probably on the phone. Whom does she spend time with? Her twin, Alice, I know that. Does she have a big family too? I have so many aunts, uncles, and cousins, all local.

Damn, it's like the more I try not to think about May, the more I think about her. Is this a forbidden-fruit deal?

I close my toolbox, satisfied with today's work. I got a good portion of the list done. I'll still need to return to go over the drywall two more times and install the rest of the light fixtures.

I walk downstairs to the delicious smell of dinner in the oven. Something with cheese and tomato, I think. My stomach growls. I only had a protein bar for lunch because I figured the faster I finished here, the better. I'll just let May know I'm going.

"May?"

She appears from the kitchen on my right. "Hey! Are you finished?"

"For now. Deer fence is fixed, some light fixtures are installed, and I patched the drywall spots, but I'll need to go over the drywall twice more and finish the lights. Two more days, and I'll be out of your hair."

"Okay, thanks so much. Let me just grab my purse."

I hold up a palm. "No payment needed."

She presses her lips together in a flat line. "I need to give you something. Free night at the inn once it's open?"

Last thing I need is to sleep close to where she's sleeping. I'll probably be up all night.

I shake my head. "No, thanks. Save it for your paying customers."

"Stay for dinner, then. There's plenty, or I could make a dish for you to go."

Sophie yells from behind me, "Stay! Have dinner with us."

I turn as Sophie bounds down the stairs, still wearing her boots, but now she's wearing warmer clothes—a long-sleeved shirt and skirt with pants underneath. She's also wearing a birthday party hat with multicolored polka dots.

"I am hungry," I admit.

"It's ziti!" Sophie exclaims. "My favorite."

"That's my favorite too. I love Italian food."

May nods once. "Great. Dinner it is." She looks between Sophie and me. Sophie's looking up at me with a wide smile, her brown eyes shining. Dad's warning about dating a single mom and how impressionable a young girl can be rings through my head.

Sophie tugs on my sleeve. "Come on, we can watch TV until dinner. I have *Twinkle Fairies* recorded."

May covers a laugh and returns to the kitchen.

Sophie's not waiting for an answer. "You're going to love them." She pulls me toward the family room in the back of the house. "My favorite is Dixie. She has the power of fire, and her hair is rainbow. My next favorite is Rose; she has the power of invisibility..."

There must be twenty fairies, and she knows each one down to the last detail. My head's spinning from the rapid input of nonessential information.

I flop down on one end of the floral sofa, and she sits cross-legged in the middle. She puts a recorded *Twinkle Fairies* on, an animated show with twinkle special effects. Sophie narrates so loudly over it that I can't hear the dialogue. Not that I want to.

When's dinner?

~

May

We eat dinner at our small rectangular kitchen table with Sophie in the middle and Mason and me at opposite ends. Mason digs into his ziti with gusto while Sophie chatters on excitedly about her favorite show, *Twinkle Fairies*. There's a different energy with Mason at the table. He seems to fill the space. I'm drawn to him, watching his expression, the way he tries to keep up with Sophie's monologue directed only at him.

Mason gives Sophie a few well-timed nods and says "uh-huh" just enough to keep Sophie satisfied. He's patient and kind.

He catches my eye, and my heart beats a little faster. "This ziti is so good. Did you train as a professional chef?"

Sophie finally returns to eating her dinner.

I smile at the compliment. "Nope, not professional. I just enjoy cooking."

"What did you do before you got into the inn business?" he asks.

"Mommy worked for a soul sucker."

I shake my head with a laugh. "I worked in a job that was soul sucking. I didn't work for a soul sucker." I turn to Mason. "I used to work in financial services. It was a lot of quarterly reports and number crunching."

He makes a face. "That does sound soul sucking. What did you want to be when you grew up?"

A mom. I keep that to myself. I love babies and little kids. "I worked as a summer camp counselor in high school and college. They always gave me the youngest group of three- and four-year-olds. They were fun and tiring at the same time. I think it gave me patience for the real thing."

He spears another ziti. "So that's what you wanted to do? Run your own summer camp?"

"Oh God no. Then you have to deal with all the demanding parents. How about you? What did you want to be when you grew up?"

He points his fork at me and gives me a knowing look. "Don't think I didn't notice you sidestepping the question. We'll circle back to that. I wanted to be a professional baseball player. So did all my brothers. We thought we'd be the first set of four brothers to make it to the major leagues."

I smile. "That would've been something. So how'd you get started on *Hot Finds*?"

"Dad was already on the show with my uncle Ty. Dad's the expert mechanic; Ty was just the host. When Ty stepped down, I stepped in. Dad taught me everything he knows. He can fix anything mechanical from a plane to a car to a motorcycle."

"Wow, a plane?" I ask.

He inclines his head. "He used to be a mechanic in the Air Force. Anyway, I love my work, and it's fun to work on the show too."

"It's great that you love your work."

Sophie eats her salad in between firing questions at Mason, wanting to know all about *Hot Finds*. Like, who picks their outfits? Does he drive the cars home really fast? How does he pick a car color?

He answers every question with a straight face with the occasional near smile breaking through. I didn't expected him to be so good with Sophie. It's nice.

After we finish, I stand to clear the dishes, and Mason helps.

When we reach the sink, he says under his breath, "She's a talker."

"Oh yeah."

Sophie appears next to Mason and looks up at him with big puppy-dog eyes. "Can I please watch you make *Hot Finds*?"

"We don't film until spring."

"He told you that already," I say. "Don't keep asking."

Sophie's shoulders fall, her expression collapsing into total devastation until she looks up again with hopeful puppy-dog eyes. "Can I see the cars on *Hot Finds*?"

I take out the tiramisu I bought for dessert. "Sophie, you see them on TV. I'm sure Mason is very busy at work." I glance at Mason. "Don't feel obligated."

He lifts his palms. "Far be it from me to turn away someone who loves cars."

"Does that mean yes?" Sophie asks.

He looks to me. "If it's okay with your mom."

Sophie gives me her best puppy-eyed look. I can't think of one good reason why we can't look at cars. It's a place of business. No big deal.

"Sure," I say. "Thank you for the invitation."

Sophie claps, then turns to me. "I'd like an extra-big piece of tiramisu, please."

"Me too," Mason says, high-fiving her.

They turn to me with matching hopeful expressions. He fits with us. What would it hurt to let him in just a little?

"You can have seconds if you're still hungry," I say.

Mason and Sophie exchange a smile, and my heart squeezes. It's easy to forget my worries about Mason when Sophie's so happy.

6

Mason

Tonight's my third and final home-cooked dinner at May's place. Everything she makes is amazing and more than suffices as a thank you. At my place, I usually get by cooking one night and eating leftovers for three days. Nothing fancy— burgers, steak, baked salmon.

I'm getting used to the high-speed-talking Sophie. Though I confess I don't listen too carefully. I'll never remember all the details she tells me about her favorite shows, school, and friends. It's like she's in a rush to tell me her life story.

May's careful not to share too much. Is it because Sophie's there? Maybe we could meet up just the two of us to talk and stuff. As friends. As long as I don't cross the line, it could work. The alternative, never spending time with her again, feels too damn hard.

After we finish an incredible chicken dish with roasted peppers and rice, I help clear the table. Sophie runs from the room, probably to watch TV. May lets her when she's busy.

"Another great dinner," I say. "You could run a five-star restaurant. Maybe that could be an add-on to the inn."

She shakes her head with a smile. "I'm providing break- fast and afternoon cookies, but beyond that is more than I can take on. I'm glad you enjoyed it. I'll walk you out."

Right. No need to linger. May was clear she wasn't looking for anything more than repairs from me. No matter how warm and friendly she's been. She's probably like that with everyone. That's why she's opening an inn.

We walk to the front door.

She smiles, but something about it seems forced. "Thanks again for all your hard work. I really appreciate it."

"You're welcome." I hesitate, not ready to say goodbye forever. "So I guess I'll go now."

She lifts a hand in a small wave.

"Unless…"

She brightens. "Yes?"

"You and Sophie could stop by the shop on Saturday to see where all the action happens for *Hot Finds*. I mean, you are fans of the show, and you said it was okay for her to check out the cars."

"Yes! Yes! Yes!" Sophie shouts, running into the foyer.

May gives me a small smile. "I guess that's a yes."

Sophie throws her arms in the air. "Woo-hoo! Can Olivia H. come too?"

"Let's just keep it us," May says.

Sophie beams at me and runs back to the family room. How long was she standing there watching our awkward goodbye?

I smile at May, and she smiles back, a real smile this time.

It won't hurt to see a friend one more time.

May

Sophie's at Sunday brunch with my parents as usual, giving me some much-needed alone time. Normally I'd relax, but today I'm restless. I don't know why. It's not like I don't have plenty of work to do for the inn. I still have to order the bedding, curtains, and all the last minute touches to make it comfortable for guests. Not to mention taking photos and getting the word out for my Valentine's Day opening.

It's just that I kinda got used to having Mason join us for dinner, and that's over. It was nice to have another adult to talk to.

The doorbell rings, and I perk up. *Is it Mason?* My pulse thrums through my veins. I smooth my hair and walk to the front door. I can't think of any reason he'd be stopping by. Unless he's thinking about me the way I keep thinking about him.

I peek through the peephole and open the door to my neighbors Mackenzie and Harper. They're Mason's cousins. Mackenzie's brown hair is up in a high ponytail, and she's wearing running clothes. Harper's honey brown hair is mostly hidden under a baseball cap, and she's got Ugg slippers on under her long coat. Sunday morning outfits.

"Hi, May, can we come in?" Mackenzie asks.

I step back. "Of course. Is there something you need?"

"Cup of sugar," Harper says.

"Oh, okay."

"She's kidding," Mackenzie says, looking around. "Wow, you've done a lot of work since the last time we were here. It looks great."

"Thank you."

"Is Sophie here?" Harper asks.

I cross my arms, already feeling protective. "She's with my parents. Why?"

Mackenzie and Harper exchange a look.

"We saw Mason leaving your house late three nights in a row," Harper says.

Mackenzie elbows her. "We're not spying. Our kitchen is in the front of the house, and we know his truck. Anyway, we're just coming to you as a friend to say..." She stops herself. "Oh, geez, we're being nosy neighbors. Sorry!"

"I'm not sorry," Harper says. "She needs to know about Aunt Madison. She's a force."

My brows scrunch together. "Mason's mom? What does she have to do with me?"

Mackenzie gives me a gentle smile. "We just wanted to

warn you, in a friendly neighborly way, that she's a fierce mama bear, so tread carefully. Her mom radar is up ever since the wedding. She's worried about the single-mom thing, you know? That Mason's not ready for that kind of responsibility." She shrugs. "Me, I say do what you want. I'm sure you're making sure to keep Sophie out of things until you know if it's serious."

I stiffen at the subtle advice on parenting my daughter. "I'm also a fierce mama bear, which is why I'm not dating *anyone*. I want to be sure Sophie doesn't get attached to someone who's not sticking around. And the last thing I want is a relationship. I'm a widow. My husband died three years ago, we were very much in love, and the thought of someone taking his place feels like a betrayal to him." My voice chokes.

"Oh, May, I'm so sorry," Mackenzie says. "I didn't know you were a widow."

"Sorry," Harper mumbles.

I glance toward the door, but neither of them seems inclined to leave.

"We should tell Aunt Madison about the widow thing," Mackenzie says to Harper.

"Good idea," Harper says. "Though I think the single-mom thing will still be an issue."

Lord save me from nosy relatives.

"We're friends," I say. "That's all. He stayed for dinner as a thank you for doing repairs on my place."

They look at me skeptically. Next thing you know, I'll get a visit from Mason's mom demanding to know my intentions toward her poor sweet boy caught in the web of a single mom.

Mackenzie studies me with concern. "I'm sure being a widow is hard, but that doesn't mean you should close yourself off to love forever."

Harper snorts. "Says the woman closed off to love."

"For this stage of my life," Mackenzie says sharply to Harper. "Like you should talk." They sure bicker like sisters.

In an attempt to end the bickering and shut down the

conversation about Mason, I go with something I've often thought about. "They say you never get over your first love. I expect that will be true for me too." Memories of Grandmom Maggie finding love again in her seventies come back to me. I push that thought away. WWMD doesn't apply here.

"God, I hope that's not true," Mackenzie says. "If my first love is my last, then there's no hope for me."

"My first love was in high school," Harper says. "Can you imagine still being with your high school boyfriend?"

"Yes," I say quietly. "My husband, Rick, and I were high school sweethearts."

"I am so sorry," Harper says.

"So sorry," Mackenzie says.

They start backing toward the door.

"It's okay." I'm used to people being uncomfortable when I talk about Rick and what I lost. I've come to terms with the loss. And part of him lives on through Sophie. He was an extrovert just like her.

"You do you, May," Harper says. "See ya."

"Bye."

Mackenzie waves with a guilty expression.

They leave, and I shut the door, leaning back against it. That was just the shakeup I needed to get back to work. No more talking about Mason; no more thinking about Mason. Just life as usual. Geez, what a nosy family he has.

I actually got a decent amount done today. I found the perfect rug for the Tranquility suite and some curtains that remind me of a summer's day, white with embroidered eyelets on the edges. Mom and Dad took Sophie to the toy store after brunch to get her another beginner jigsaw puzzle. Of course the toy store can take a long time. Sophie loves just about everything in there.

The front door opens with a flurry of activity and noise. My parents are back with Sophie. They have a key.

I close my laptop and welcome Sophie with open arms. She runs to me and gives me a hug. I sigh, breathing in the sweet scent of her hair. She still uses the no-tear baby shampoo.

I pull back to look at her. "Did you have fun?"

"Yes! I had silver-dollar pancakes with whipped cream, and I got a fairy puzzle with thirty-two pieces. It says for seven and up, but Grandmom says I'm smart enough to figure it out." She sheds her coat and hat, dropping them on the floor.

Mom gestures to the lower hooks on the wall with a stern look. Sophie puts her coat and hat on the hooks without complaint. Mom's a retired third grade teacher, but she's still got the magic touch.

I smile at my parents, a study in contrasts. Mom's blond with blue eyes and an optimist. Dad has caramel brown hair with hazel eyes, and he's a pragmatist. I took more after him in looks. I consider myself a cautious optimist. "Thanks for the puzzle. Great winter activity." I look down at Sophie. "Did you say thank you to Grandmom and Grandpop?"

"Ye-e-es," she says dramatically. All that's missing is the eye roll for a peek at teenage Sophie.

I was fortunate to grow up with two loving parents who supported me and Alice in all things, even when Alice went through her Buddhist monk phase and took a vow of silence. We were fourteen and had just learned about monks in school. Anyway, the only person she was silent in front of were Mom and Dad. She talked at school and whispered to me in our shared bedroom. Through the whole thing, Mom and Dad made sealed-lips gestures, knowing nods, and smiles when she didn't answer a question. They communicated with her by note. I hope I can be that patient when Sophie's a teen.

Mom hands Sophie the puzzle, folding the plastic bag from the store into neat squares.

Dad holds his hand out to Sophie. "Here, I'll help you open it."

She hands him the puzzle, and he pulls out his ever-present multiuse pocketknife from his pocket and breaks the seal along the edges.

Sophie grabs it. "Thanks, Grandpop!" She runs into the living room.

Dad follows. "I'll help you open the bag of pieces."

"Okay! But I'm doing the puzzle all by myself."

"You got it, Sophie the Great."

She giggles.

Mom turns to me, saying in a low voice, "All she could talk about was Mason the Great. He can fix anything; he's a TV star; he loves Mommy. How come this is the first time I'm hearing about him?"

I sigh. Sophie's hoping for something that won't happen. I'll have a talk with her after my parents leave.

I meet Mom's eyes. "Because there was nothing to say. He fixed some stuff around here. I know Sophie might want there to be more to the story, but Mason and I are just friends."

"Sophie says you went to a wedding with him, he stayed for dinner three times, and you're going to see *Hot Finds*."

"Where they film *Hot Finds*," I correct. "And, yes, I fed him dinner as a thank you for the free repairs. And the wedding was a spur-of-the-moment thing because Sophie wanted to dance and have cake."

She gives me a skeptical look. "That sounds like more than friends. All this happened in a week. It sounds like the start of something." She points at me. "Oh, and Sophie said he could tell you and Alice apart when you wore the same black dress. He passed the test."

I close my eyes for a moment. Isn't Sophie just a fire hose of information? I need to be careful what she's privy to.

Dad walks over, smiling. "She sure likes that puzzle."

Mom turns to him. "May says she and Mason are just friends, but they're seeing each other an awful lot."

"If May says they're just friends, I believe her," Dad says. "May, didn't you say after things didn't work out with Oliver the Cheater last year, you would never date again?"

"Yes. At least, not until Sophie's in college."

He smiles, looking pleased. "See, Liz, nothing to worry about."

Mom clenches her teeth. "I'm *not* worried, Ryan." She turns to me with a bright smile. "I want to meet him. Invite him over for dinner at our house next Sunday."

Danger! Mama-bear alert! Mom won't hesitate to ask Mason all the hard questions: What are your intentions? Are you the kind who loves them and leaves them? May is very special, blah, blah, blah. Embarrassing but true. She means well. I'm sure I'll be much more chill when Sophie starts dating. My heart lurches. Sophie dating? Staying out at all hours? Not knowing where she is? No, no, no. Plenty of time before the teenaged years.

I glance at Dad, who grimaces. He won't contradict Mom, but he sees as clearly as I do that inviting Mason to meet them for a family dinner is a *ridiculous* idea.

"I'll make a roast," Mom says.

"Mom, no. I'm not inviting him to dinner."

"Then I'll go with you to *Hot Finds* to meet him. That's neutral ground."

I turn to Dad with a beseeching look.

He shrugs. "It's better than dinner, isn't it?"

I throw my hands in the air. "This is insane. We're just friends. I probably won't even see him again after we visit his shop."

"I'll pop in like I'm interested in a car," Mom says. "You can introduce me, and I'll pop out. I'm a fan of the show too."

"You are not."

She lifts her chin. "I could be after visiting the set. Much more interesting to see cars in real life than on TV." She turns to Dad. "Right?"

"Sure."

Mom squeezes my arm. "Sophie's crazy about him. Once I meet him, I'll know right away if he's a good fish or one to throw away."

I frown. One week and Sophie's crazy about him. "I don't

want her to get attached. Maybe I should cancel our visit to his shop."

"Don't cancel," Dad says. "Sophie's excited to see the cars. Hell, I wouldn't mind checking out the classic cars myself."

"You can't both show up," I say in exasperation.

"What? I'm a fan," Dad says.

Mom smiles at him and turns to me. "Just I'll go. Then it won't be embarrassing."

Right. Not embarrassing at all. But at least it's not a family dinner. Dad's laid-back, but he can still pull a serious cop demeanor that's pretty intense. He was the chief of police here in Clover Park for years.

I cave. "Fine. As long as you understand it's a friend thing."

She pats my arm. "Of course, sweetheart."

Mom gathers her purse and coat. Having achieved her goal, she's leaving before I can change my mind. Dad notices she's dressed and ready to go, so he puts his coat on too.

"Bye." I hug Mom and then Dad.

They say bye to Sophie, and she runs over, hugs them, and runs back to her puzzle.

Mom steps out the door first and turns back a moment later, holding a Something's Brewing Café bakery bag. She hands it to me. "There's a note on the receipt."

Did Mason bring me baked goods? I mean *us*. That's so thoughtful. I turn the bag around to read the note: Sorry! Your nosy neighbors, M and H

I open the bag and find two chocolate-frosted donuts. That was nice. Mackenzie and Harper were just trying to warn me about Mason's mom. I won't be warning him about my mom. I don't want to get into why she wants to meet him. Anyway, I find it hard to believe that Mason's mom would show up here, even if she is fierce.

Dad joins Mom, car keys in hand.

Mom looks at me curiously. "What are your neighbors sorry about?"

"Don't ask."

"I just did."

Dad puts his arm around Mom. "Let her have at least one secret from her parents." He guides her away, and she cranes her neck to look at me again.

I wave. "Later! Love you!"

"Love you too, May Bear."

I stifle a groan and shut the door. Then I send up a silent prayer that she won't call me May Bear in front of Mason. And I thought his family was nosy.

7

———

When I pull into the parking lot of Exotic and Classic Restorations, two things stand out at once—they're closed on Saturdays, and both Mason and Mom are already here. She's early! Has she already talked his ear off about my childhood shenanigans? Shown him baby pictures? Until Sophie was born, Mom kept a picture of me and Alice when we were two as her phone screensaver. We were naked except for diapers, wearing our swimsuits on our heads to be funny. Not so funny once you're past the diaper stage.

As soon as I park, Sophie rushes out of the car. I grab her hand, lock the door, and hurry over to Mom's car, hoping she's still in there. Her familiar blond head comes into view.

"Grandmom!" Sophie yells, breaking free of my hand and running to the driver's side.

Well, at least there wasn't any embarrassing talk or picture viewing behind my back. I can still control the situation.

Mom gets out of the car and picks up Sophie, hugging her. Sophie pulls back to look at her. "Today's going to be awesome!"

Mom smiles and sets her down. "I think so too. Let's look around while your mom tells Mason we're here."

"Okay!"

The two of them wander the lot, where classic cars in need of repair wait. There's three garage bays at the shop with a car in each. I peek into the bays, but don't see Mason in there.

I ring the bell on the front door of the showroom, where classic cars gleam with shiny chrome and fresh paint jobs. This must be where they sell the classic cars they find. I can never remember the names of the cars, probably because I'm so distracted by Mason talking about them.

I cup my hands on the glass, looking for my favorite from last season, a convertible done in silver and turquoise. Grandmom Maggie was partial to convertibles too. We have that in common, even though I'm not nearly as adventurous. Sometimes I wish I were. Maybe when Sophie's in college, I'll get myself a convertible to ride around in.

Mason's face appears suddenly close-up on the other side of the glass. I jump back, my heart racing. How did he sneak up on me like that?

He opens the door and steps out with a grin. "Gotcha."

"Were you crouching down so you could suddenly pop up?"

"I came from the service hallway, saw you peeking, and moved fast to surprise you. No crouching. You were just so focused. Thinking about buying a car?"

"No, thanks. I need practical and reliable like my good old Honda." I lower my voice as Mom and Sophie approach. "So, uh, my mom wanted to meet you. No big. Probably just curious about a local celebrity. She won't stay long."

"I had no idea so many women watched the show," he says in wonder. "Even had a superfan show up here this morning. I told her only by invitation and sent her on her way."

"A woman fan showed up here unannounced? Does that happen often?"

"Just with her."

I stare at him for a moment, concerned. That doesn't sound right.

Objectively speaking, he's gorgeous with the kind of muscled body women want to feel pressed against them. Maybe this woman hopes to catch his interest through sheer persistence. I bet she's beautiful. My jaw clenches. I bet he has legions of beautiful women fans dying to be with him.

I'm *not* jealous.

"Hello!" Mom calls as they approach.

Sophie runs to us and beams up at Mason. "It's just like on TV."

"Pretty much." Mason holds his hand out to Mom. "Mason Shaw, nice to meet you."

"Liz O'Hare. I'm a fan of your show."

Sophie's head snaps to Mom's. "You said you never saw it."

Mom smiles guiltily. "You, Grandpop, and your mom are fans, so that makes me a fan by association."

"Oh," Sophie says.

I barely hold back an eye roll.

Mason laughs. "Okay, well, let me show you around." He opens the garage bay to show us a pink Cadillac.

"A pink car!" Sophie exclaims.

It *is* beautiful, shiny pink and chrome. I peer into the driver's side window, admiring the pink leather interior with white trim and the old-fashioned dials on the dashboard.

Mason describes the restoration process they went through to get the car in shape. It's almost like we're watching his show.

"We even found a pink Cadillac keychain to surprise the client with." He lifts it off the counter to show us. "This one's ready to go. She'll pick it up on Monday." He walks to the next bay and gestures for us to follow.

The next car is up on a lift. It has no wheels, and the sides are gray and rusty. Mason gestures toward it. "Chevy Corvette. Not much to look at, but we'll give it a new life."

"Will it be pink?" Sophie asks.

"Cherry red."

"I like cherries."

Mason nods. "And over here is a Jaguar E-Type. It's an awesome car, but always breaking down. Not easy to get the parts either."

I want it. It's a beautiful sky blue convertible. Probably too expensive, especially with a daughter in college. I'm practical about money, even in my fantasies for future me.

I notice an orange sign on the wall that says Road Machinery Ahead. "That's the sign we always see on the show."

Mason inclines his head. "Yeah. We usually film in that bay. We have to empty all three bays for the camera and crew with all their gear. We temporarily store cars in a garage in back." He takes us all in. "Any questions?"

"Can I sit in the pink car?" Sophie asks.

I shake my head. "Sophie, no. That's someone else's car."

"How about I give you a ride in it?" Mason asks. "If that's okay with your mom."

"Can I, Mom?"

"As long as you wear your seatbelt."

She nods and smiles, running to the car.

"You're both welcome too. The back seat's nice and roomy," Mason says.

"I'm okay," I say. "Thanks."

Mom nods. "I'll stay with May."

"Okay. I'll just drive once around the building," Mason says to me.

"Thank you for humoring her," I say.

One corner of his mouth turns up. "Hard to turn down a car afficionado's request."

Mason presses a button to open the garage bay. Sophie's already in the passenger seat, putting on her seatbelt. Mason gets in the driver's side, starts it, and eases the car out of the bay.

As soon as they pull out, Mom says to me, "You didn't mention he was a major hottie."

"Mom, please don't say hottie."

"Why not?"

"It just sounds weird coming from you."

"It's obvious. No wonder you're a fan of his car show."

I walk outside, hoping she doesn't see the flush to my cheeks. She joins me. The pink Cadillac makes a slow turn around the building. Mason's pointing and talking, giving Sophie more of the tour.

"He's good with her," she says.

"He's just being polite."

She gives me a searching look. "If you want me to look after Sophie so you two can go out—"

I put a hand up. "It's not like that."

"Okay, okay. Though I'm not sure why not."

"I'm just not ready for dating. The one time I tried was a disaster. I take that as a sign that I'm not meant for a relationship."

She gives me a sympathetic look. "Rick set the bar high."

"Exactly. Besides, I've got too much going on right now to juggle one more thing."

She smooths my hair back. "I know you're busy, honey, and I know you miss Rick. We all do. But there are people who make your load lighter instead of adding to it."

I think about Mason doing all those repairs for free, taking a big weight off my shoulders so I could focus more on the fun part of decorating the rooms and figuring out marketing ideas.

The pink Cadillac appears again. Mason backs it into the bay, gets out, and tosses the keys on the counter.

Sophie pops out of the car. "It's like riding in a boat! It glides."

Mason gestures toward the showroom. "Would you like to go inside?"

"Sure," I say. "We always see it on the show. You must sell every car that's on TV."

He grins. "We do. Best advertising, and they pay us to do the show."

"That's a good deal," I say.

Mason holds open the interior door from the bay to the showroom, and Sophie races through. Mom and I follow at a slower pace.

While Sophie rushes from car to car, peeking in all the cars' windows, Mom takes the opportunity to interrogate Mason. Good thing I didn't chase after Sophie. Now I can control the conversation before she shares too much about me.

Mom smiles serenely before saying sweetly, "So, Mason, where did you grow up? I don't recall seeing you or your family before."

"Right here in Eastman."

Drawing him in before the kill.

"Mmm, that explains it," Mom says. "I know most of the kids who went through the Clover Park school system. And how do you feel about your mother, do you have any sisters, and do you have a criminal record?"

Whoa! Too far. "Mom! You can't accuse him of being a criminal."

Mom leans toward Mason, speaking in a conspiratorial tone. "May's dad was the chief of police, so it's best to know these things up front. I do believe in redemption."

Mason opens his mouth, but nothing comes out.

Kill me now. Also, since when has Mom been cool with me dating a former criminal? Is she that determined for me to find someone? I bet it's because Alice and Charlie are blissfully happy together, always laughing and talking about their latest travel adventure. Not that I'm jealous. It's just an unfair comparison.

"Dad's retired," I tell Mason.

"You didn't answer my questions," Mom says to Mason.

"You don't have to," I say.

Mason nods at me, then says to mom, "My mom rocks, total badass, no sisters, three brothers though, and no, I don't have a criminal record."

Mom clasps her hands together like he's the answer to her

prayer. "That is great news, Mason. I won't hold the no-sister thing against you."

"Thank you?" he says uncertainly.

Mom firmly believes that a man with a sister understands women better. My dad grew up with two brothers. Mom always says he had a learning curve. Ha.

Mom smiles at me. "I'll get out of your hair now." She turns to Mason. "So nice meeting you."

"You too."

She leaves. He stares out the front window, looking a bit dazed.

"Sorry," I say. "It's so embarrassing when family butts in. I guess you know all about that with your cousins."

He cocks his head. "Which cousins?"

"Mackenzie and Harper. They stopped by my house the other day to warn me about your mom."

Yet another reason not to get involved with Mason. If it didn't work out, I'd be stuck living across the street from his crazy family, who might hold it against me. My home is my business, and the last thing I need is problems with the neighbors.

He stares blankly for a moment. "Warn you about my mom? Why?"

"I said too much. Clearly, this is news to you, and you should ask your cousins."

"Oh, I will." He sounds irritated.

I try to lighten up the conversation. "I guess you noticed Mom's kinda quirky. So was my grandmom Maggie, but they're not blood related. It runs on both sides. I couldn't help but turn out quirky."

He leans in. "How are you quirky?"

My breath catches in my throat. I wave a hand airily. "Oh, you know, because I quit a well-paying job to open an inn. Don't get me wrong, I crunched the numbers, and I have savings to tide us over for what I hope will be a short time. But most people at my company would never do something so different from number crunching like opening an inn. They're financial services lifers, climbing that corporate ladder."

"That's not quirky. That's following your dream."

I rub a hand on the side of my neck. "And I also talk to myself out loud and forget sometimes to stop when I'm in public."

He grins. "You do? Like where?"

"The supermarket, Sophie's school, the inn."

"But the inn's your home."

"I forget sometimes I'm talking to myself in front of the contractors."

He looks intrigued. "What else?"

"I need the label of everything to be facing front, cans, bottles, whatever. I have to have it all lined up and looking pretty."

"Pretty?"

I warm to my subject. "And my spices are in alphabetical order. Though I admit that one's because Mom's super neat and organized. Growing up, it just seemed like that's how things were supposed to be."

"Our house was messy and loud. I think I would've liked your house better so I could hear myself think."

I laugh. "It wasn't quiet. Alice and I were energetic, excitable kids like Sophie. Wait. Where is Sophie?"

I scan the showroom and don't see her dark head of hair. My heart picks up speed as I weave through cars in search of her. Maybe she's lying in the back seat of one. "Sophie? Where are you?"

Mason searches the other side of the showroom.

Seven cars. No Sophie.

I race out the front door and stop short. "Oh my God."

"Did you…" Mason trails off.

Sophie drives by in the pink Cadillac. She's standing, clutching the steering wheel as she drives way too fast toward the parking lot.

I run after her, waving my arms. A field is behind the lot, a road on the other side. Please don't turn.

"Sophie!" I yell. "Hit the brakes! Step on the other pedal."

The driver's side window is down, so she hears me. The car jerks to a stop, and then she moves forward again, turning toward the road.

My heart's in my throat. "Sophie! Stop! Stop!"

In my peripheral vision, I see Mason sprint past me. He gets in the passenger side of the Cadillac, takes the wheel, and turns away from the road. They slow and then speed up. Is Sophie interfering? They do a screeching donut and finally come to a slow stop a few feet ahead of that.

I put a hand on my thundering heart. I just lost ten years off my life.

What the hell was she thinking? She could've been seriously hurt. I know she wasn't wearing a seatbelt standing in the driver's seat. And she stole a car!

Does she know how much she scared me?

I walk over on shaking legs as the adrenaline leaves my body. I'm her mom. It's my job to keep her safe. I was distracted by Mason and didn't keep an eye on her. Guilt floods me. She's only five. She needs watching. Just one more reason not to get involved with Mason. I can't afford to be distracted from my primary responsibility.

Time for a Stern Lecture. I gear up for what I'm going to say as I march over.

When I get to the car, Mason's talking to Sophie in a firm voice about safety and how important it is for her mom to know she's safe and her grandmom and everyone who loves her.

"Like you?" Sophie asks.

"Uh, sure. So you won't do that again, right? Not until you're old enough to drive a car."

How can he be so calm? I take a few steps away, trying to get my breathing to steady. My hands are shaking, and my legs feel like jelly.

Mason notices me. "Hey. Just telling her about personal safety and driver's licenses."

My heart cracks open for just a moment at his gentle calm demeanor during a crisis. Then I look at my daughter and lose it. She could've died! "Sophie, get out of the car! We're leaving now, and we're going to have a serious talk about this! And no TV for a month!"

She slinks out of the car, her shoulders slumped.

"Sophie, you owe Mason an apology for taking his client's car out."

"Sorry," Sophie says in a small voice.

"I'll forgive you as long as you swear on Hornbow that you'll never do that again."

She nods solemnly. "I swear on Hornbow."

"Go get in the car," I tell Sophie, pointing to it. "I'll be there in a minute." It's not far from where I'm standing. I watch her get in the car before turning to Mason.

"I'm so sorry. I'll pay for whatever damage she's done."

He pockets the keys. "Nah, it's fine. I'll give it a fresh polish, and it'll be good to go." He searches my expression. "You're trembling. C'mere."

He opens his arms to me, and I don't hesitate, stepping into his arms and hugging him tight. His strong arms wrap around me, steadying my world.

After a long moment, I pull away, wiping my eyes. "Thanks."

"Anytime."

Our gazes meet and hold with an intensity that tells me I can no longer ignore what I'm feeling for him. I want to spend more time with this man. "Would you like to have dinner with me tonight just the two of us?"

His voice is husky. "I'd like that very much. This time I'll make it. You can come to my place."

"Great," I say.

"Great," he says.

We stand there smiling at each other. A rush of affection goes through me, and I spontaneously hug him again.

When I pull away, he squeezes both my hands gently. "Seven good?"

"Seven's awesome."

I walk back to my car in a daze.

Sophie pipes up from the back seat. "I saw you hugging Mason."

"Yes. We're going to have a grown-up dinner tonight."

"What's a grown-up dinner?"

I pull out of the lot. "It's the kind where you only talk about boring grown-up things and eat a lot of vegetables."

"Oh. I don't think I want to grow up, then."

I look at her in the rearview mirror. "You've got plenty of time."

"I know all about how babies are made," she says matter-of-factly, shocking me speechless. I swear I'm going to go prematurely gray because of her.

"Hmm…well, it seems we have a lot to talk about, starting with how you never, ever drive a car. You could've gotten seriously hurt!"

"Sorry, Mommy."

"And I was really scared. I don't know what I'd do if anything happened to you. Promise you'll never do anything like that again."

"I promise. I love you, Mommy."

I let out a breath. "I love you too."

I put on her favorite kids' music and stare wide-eyed out the window. Sex talk. Not what I expected on the way home. This will take some careful thought. And nerves of steel.

"I want a baby sister," she says.

It's going to be a long car ride.

"Let's play the quiet game." My little trick to see how long I can keep her quiet. She's gotten better at it.

I relax a little. I have something to look forward to tonight, dinner with Mason just the two of us at his place. Am I really ready to take this step? Can I let go of my inhibitions for once and enjoy the most gorgeous sexy man I've been fantasizing about ever since I discovered his show?

But is that wanting a fantasy and not the man?

Am I really considering a fling just for fun? My heart races at the thought. Exciting, wild, carefree fun. So not me, but practically speaking, it seems the safest route. No complications or hurt feelings.

The problem is, I'm not sure there is a safe route where Mason's concerned.

8

Mason

I've got it all covered for the gift trifecta—wine, flowers, and chocolate. My pulse thrums. Just the two of us at my place. What does it mean to her? Is this a date or casual sex? It's possible it's been a while for her, and she said she didn't date, so…

The doorbell rings, followed by the ding of the oven timer. "Coming!" I yell before grabbing the oven mitts and taking the enchiladas out of the oven. It's one of two dinners I make that are good enough to serve to a woman. The other is lasagna. I don't make them often since they're so much work, and I'm usually too hungry to wait that long for dinner. May deserves the best I can give her.

The bell rings again. Shit. She didn't hear me. I run to the door and fling it open. "Sorry, I had to take dinner out of the oven. Wait right there!"

I race back to the dining room to get the flowers and chocolate. Wine can wait for dinner.

May steps inside, wearing a snug blue dress that clings to her sexy curves. Her hair falls in a silky cascade of caramel brown. My mouth goes dry. I just stand there staring, holding my gifts.

She laughs a little. "Is that for me?"

"We could share the wine. It's in the dining room." I hand her the flowers and candy. "Yes, it's all for you."

"Thank you, Mason. This is really nice."

"Sure. Take a seat in the dining room."

She looks around my place. I have a two-story colonial home in Eastman that I bought with the *Hot Finds* money. It's not decorated all that much. Brown leather furniture with a wooden coffee table. Glossy pictures of classic cars hang in black frames on the wall.

She gestures toward my photos. "Are these all from *Hot Finds?*"

"Some are. Some are clients' cars we restored or cars I dream of owning."

"I'd like a convertible one day."

"Yeah, what kind?"

"Sky blue like the one in your bay. Jaguar."

I whistle. "That's a pricey one."

She waves that away. "Just a fantasy."

I stand there for a moment, dazed by her beauty. "I'll bring dinner in."

"I'll help."

"You're the guest."

She follows me into the kitchen, which is a disaster zone—sauce splatters, cheese shreds, and dirty dishes.

I throw my arms out. "You weren't supposed to see this. Go to the dining room and pretend it's magic how dinner appeared on the table."

She laughs, her hand touching my arm. A good sign.

I bring everything to the dining room. The table is set for two with wineglasses.

May smiles at me, and my heart thumps harder. "The flowers are lovely. So cheerful."

I gesture vaguely toward the living room. "They were the best in the shop, besides the red roses, but that didn't seem appropriate for the occasion." I study her. "Or maybe they were?"

Her cheeks flush. She grabs her purse from the back of her

chair and pulls out a small envelope. "Before I forget, Sophie wanted me to give you this."

I open the envelope. It's an invitation to Sophie's sixth birthday party.

I look up. "It's tomorrow."

May sighs. "She didn't think it was fair that she didn't get to see you for dinner. She wanted to invite you to her birthday party so she could see you too. I'll tell her you're busy."

It's a big deal when a kid invites you to their birthday party. It's like their holiday.

Of course, May didn't have to let Sophie invite me. Does this mean May wants me to be a part of their life? Like a relationship? I like her a lot, think about her way too much, but am I ready for the complication of a kid in the mix?

I put the invitation to the side, so no food gets on it. Wanting some time to think, I stand and pick up the wine and corkscrew, opening the bottle. I pour red wine into both our glasses and serve the enchiladas. There's salad, too, just for her.

She smiles. "Thanks. This looks delicious." She waves the steam from the enchilada. "I'll start with the salad."

I sip wine. I need to give May an answer about the birthday party since it's tomorrow. So much pressure riding on one invitation. Am I in or out? Dad's warning about being ready to commit so I don't hurt mom or daughter runs through my head once again. I wish it didn't have to be so complicated. May's the first woman I've met in a long while whom I really click with. I look at the invitation as if it holds the answer.

"Don't even worry about the party," May says. "You'd have a terrible time. Picture twelve noisy six-year-old girls high on sugar racing around my house. They're playing Twinkle Fairies, pin the tail on the unicorn, and then I arranged for a karaoke machine. It'll be noisy, you'll probably lose some hearing from all the high-pitched squeals and shouting and, truthfully, she'll be so involved with her friends she won't notice if you're there or not. No big deal. Really."

Now I get the feeling May doesn't want me to go. Does that mean she doesn't want me in her life?

"Would I be the only adult there?" I ask.

"My mom and sister will be there to try to keep some order. At least until Alice gets a migraine. She can't take the noise of a group of kids for long. So, you see, we're all set." She spears a piece of lettuce.

I slice off a piece of enchilada. "Do you not want me to go to Sophie's party?"

May smiles sweetly. "I want what you want. No pressure."

I relax. It's just a party. It doesn't have to mean a commitment. We can take things slow, see where they go. Right? It doesn't have to be as complicated as I'm making it out to be.

Our gazes meet. Her lips part.

Lust surges through me. My voice comes out hoarse. "Okay if I go to the party?"

"Yes," she says on a sigh before pulling me close and kissing me. Her lips are soft and yielding. I deepen the kiss, sliding a hand in her hair, loving the feel of her. Suddenly May takes over, hot and demanding, and I rev to rock-hard lust in an instant. I slide my hands to her sides, ready to pull her into my lap, when she jerks away.

Dazed from the loss, I stare at her blankly.

She gives me a tight smile. "Don't want dinner to get cold."

Follow her lead.

But I'm so revved up.

What was that?

I take a sip of wine, and she does the same. My God, I want her. I've never wanted anyone more in my life. From one kiss!

"May?"

"Yeah?"

"Is this a date, or is this more like casual..." I stop myself from saying sex. Instead I gesture up and down my body.

She laughs and cuts off a piece of enchilada, popping it in her mouth.

Which is not an answer.

~

May

He kissed me. Or I kissed him. I'm not sure who went first but wow. A shock of excitement went through me at first touch, and then I just wanted to climb his body and ravish him. That scared the hell out of me, so I slammed on the brakes. I'm not one to rush to the bedroom.

I glance over at him as we finish up dinner. He told me about his big noisy family. And here I thought my family held the record for nuttiest people. His mom went to her prom as Darth Vader for one, his uncle Josh and aunt Hailey had a frenemy war that people still talk about, and he and his brothers nearly killed each other growing up, "all in good fun," as they wrestled and explored the woods. I shudder to think of managing four rowdy boys. Just one girl is exhausting.

He sets his fork down. "Would you like dessert?"

My breath catches, his dark eyes intent on mine. Is dessert sex?

His gaze drops to my lips, and I desperately want him to kiss me again.

"Yes." My voice sounds throaty.

He stands, and I stare at his broad manly chest. My pulse skitters. Does he think this is casual sex too? I never answered him before when he said date or casual, but I can't let myself get serious about another man. Rick was my first and last love. It's safer that way.

He passes by me and goes to the other room. Am I supposed to follow him? I smooth my hair and pop a breath mint.

He returns a moment later, carrying the box of chocolates from Shane's Sweets he gave me earlier. Ah. He meant actual dessert. I'm craving him not dessert. I just have to let him know. Right? Sophie's spending the night at Alice's place. This is the ideal time.

He opens the box and sets it in front of me. "You first."

I chicken out. "Thanks." I pick a chocolate that looks promising, round like maybe it has a cherry inside. I pop the chocolate in my mouth, and a rich chocolate ganache with a hint of cherry brings a moment of pure bliss. "Mmm."

He stares at my mouth. I lick my lips. He turns back to the box, picks out one, and then feeds it to me. I flush hot, enjoying the chocolate while delicious anticipation races through me. But then his brows knit together like he's thinking hard. His serious expression makes me think he's about to be a gentleman and say goodnight. I'm losing my chance! I need to make a move!

I stand abruptly. "Do you want to go upstairs?"

He's quiet.

Oh great. I finally make a move on a guy first, and he's not into it. This is so freaking embarrassing. Do I sit down again or run out the door? There's no taking it back. It's just out there. An unreturned *I want you.*

Finally, he says something. "I want you too, but are you sure?"

He must be worried about the fact that I come with strings. I can do the casual thing. I've wanted him from the moment I saw him on TV. Meeting him in real life took the attraction to a whole 'nother level.

"It doesn't have to mean anything," I say with a smile.

He takes my hand, his thumb brushing lightly against the inside of my wrist. The sensitive skin tingles.

He stands, his eyes hot on mine as he shifts close. My heart thumps harder. He wraps an arm around my waist and with a quick tug makes me tip into him. My entire body softens as his body presses against mine.

His warm hand cups the back of my neck. A shiver of

excitement races down my spine. He shifts, speaking near my ear, his breath hot against my skin. "So you want casual sex?"

The word *sex* coming out of his mouth shoots straight through me. I throb. "God, yes."

He kisses me urgently, setting off a fire of desire. I clutch his shoulders as he palms my ass, pulling me up on tiptoe against him. His hard desire pressed right where I need it most makes me let go. I lose myself in the feel of his mouth claiming mine. The kiss goes on and on, consuming me, making me ache. I lift a leg, wrapping it around his. I need more. Much more.

He breaks the kiss and takes my hand, his voice low and husky. "Be sure, May. This is a line we can't uncross."

I'll probably never see him again after this, which means it doesn't matter.

"Let's cross all the lines tonight," I say.

With a sound that's between a growl and a groan, he scoops me up and carries me upstairs. This is better than any fantasy I've had about him.

I let my dress fall to the floor, wearing only a blue lacy bra with matching panties. Oh yes, I prepared for this possibility, veering from enthusiastic to sensible for the entire two hours it took me to get ready.

His gaze rakes over me before he closes the distance, cradling my face in his warm hands. "May, you're so beautiful."

I'm not perfect. I've had a baby, and I don't work out much, but in that moment I feel beautiful. "Thank you."

He gazes into my eyes. "Thank *you*." His lips meet mine, softly grazing one way and then another before settling over mine. I nearly sigh; the sensation is so delicious. One long kiss follows another as desire pools between my legs.

I press harder against him, needing more. He nips my bottom lip, shocking me. Then he claims my mouth, his hands stroking all over my body—my shoulders, my back, my hips. He holds my hips, his thumbs stroking in wide arcs that make me crazed, rocking against him. He cups my ass, pressing me against him right where I need it.

I grab his shirt and pull. "Get this stuff off."

He complies with satisfying speed while I toss my bra and panties to the side. Then he's on me, his arms wrapped around me, kissing me as he backs me up toward the bed. My knees hit the mattress. He pulls back the comforter and lifts me effortlessly onto the center of the bed.

I open my legs to him and belatedly remember protection. "Condom."

"Not yet." He kisses me, settling himself next to me while his hand skates up my side before finally caressing my breast. His thumb strokes my nipple, and I moan into his mouth. He breaks the kiss, lowering his body to taste and suckle my hard nipple. I thread my fingers through his hair, lost in sensation. He caresses the other breast before shifting to give it the same treatment.

I reach for him, but he pushes my hand away.

His voice is low and raw. "You first." His mouth covers mine as his hand slides down my body, heading in a straight line to pleasure central. And when he finally touches me, my hips arch toward him. *Oh yes.* His fingers are amazing. I don't even care how he's so good at this. My hips rock to his rhythm as tension coils tight inside me.

He breaks the kiss, gazing hotly at me while he strokes faster. My breath comes harder as the intensity escalates, carrying me higher and higher. His mouth grazes along the cord of my neck before biting down just hard enough to shock me. My entire body arches, and then he pushes me over the edge in an explosion of pleasure. He stays with me, stroking gently, easing me through wave after wave of sensation until I'm spent.

I smile dreamily, reaching for him.

He grins, rolls a condom on, and joins me, entering slowly, filling me. This feels so good, so right. I wrap my legs around him and kiss him passionately. That sets off a wild thrill ride as he rocks into me with deep, hard thrusts. Pleasure escalates once more, only more intense. White hot with each stroke. I tremble, and then I break, rocking helplessly as he takes me over the edge and keeps going, pounding into me. My nails dig into his shoulders through a pleasure so intense it overwhelms. He lets go with a hoarse sound, pumping into me, rocking me with aftershocks.

He finally stills and holds me tight against him while we catch our breath. He lifts his head, gives me a tender kiss, and rolls to his back.

I stare at the ceiling, still breathless and dazed. "Wow."

"Yeah, wow."

Mason rolls out of bed and heads to the bathroom. I guess this is the part where I'm supposed to get dressed and leave. Pretty sure that's how it goes when it's casual.

He returns and pulls on his boxer briefs.

I'm not sure what to say afterwards in the casual-sex game since I've never played it before. I go with good manners. "Thanks."

He climbs back into bed, grinning. "Thanks?"

"I mean, that was fantastic."

He props up on an elbow, looking down at me. His deep brown eyes seem to see all my vulnerable places. He brushes my hair back, his finger tracing my cheek down to the sensitive skin under my ear. "What made you change your mind about being more than friends?"

He's gorgeous, sexy, kind, generous, sweet. I can't say all that mushy stuff. This is supposed to be casual.

"You make me feel good."

He smiles. "You make me feel good too."

I prop up on my elbows, gathering the energy to get out of bed. "I'll get going now. Tonight was exactly what I needed."

He smiles. "A helluva first date."

I sit up, and he surprises me, cupping his hand on the back of my neck and kissing along my jawline up to my ear. "So no second date? We can start all over right now." His hand slides to my inner thigh, and every nerve ending stands at attention.

"Another dinner?" I ask cheekily.

He pulls me under him, and I lose myself to long, languid kisses from a man who takes his time.

9

Mason

Someone's shaking my shoulder. I'm sprawled on my stomach, my face buried in a pillow that smells like vanilla. Now someone's pulling my shoulder. I shake them off. Five more minutes.

"Mason, wake up! We overslept, and someone's at your door."

I turn my head, opening one eye. *May.* I smile.

Last night.

Incredible.

I reach for her, but she pushes me away. "Go answer your door. I have to get home before Sophie and get ready for her party."

Another dinging of the doorbell, followed by urgent knocking. I glance at the clock on the nightstand. Eight fifteen a.m. on a Sunday. No one I know would show up at this hour. Unless it was an emergency. Adrenaline shoots through me. I pull on jeans from yesterday and throw on a T-shirt.

May's just about dressed. I want to say bye, but I have to deal with whoever's out there first. Please don't let anyone be dead.

I pull the door open to find my superfan, Evie, on my doorstep. She's young, blond, damn persistent. You know, I suspected she'd followed me from home when she left a note on my truck at the pizzeria. Damn, I should've filed a restraining order. "Evie, you can't be here."

"You never called me. I told you it was important."

May appears next to me, staring at Evie. "Excuse me."

"Wait a minute," I say to her.

Evie holds her hand out to May. "I'm Evie. Did Mason tell you about me?"

May looks to me in question.

"She's a fan of the show. I met her one time when she showed up at Happy Endings."

"He forgot the important part," Evie says smugly. "We drank tequila, and then we hooked up in his truck. Mason, I'm pregnant, and you're the father."

I blow out a breath, annoyed. "I wasn't drunk that night. You had tequila while I had a beer. And we did *not* hook up."

"I can't believe you don't remember!" she cries. "How many women do you sleep with in a night?"

May puts a hand on my arm. "This seems like a private conversation. Excuse me, I need to get home."

"May, she's just a crazy fan," I say. "I barely know her."

She recoils. "Shame on you. You at least owe Evie a conversation about this."

"Yeah!" Evie says. "Shame on you. I'm sure it's a boy, and I'm going to name him Mason after you."

May darts out the door.

"I'll see you at Sophie's party later!" I call to her rapidly retreating back.

"Don't bother!" she yells.

I want to yell I don't have drunken hookups with random strangers, but just then my elderly neighbor next door comes out in her bathrobe to pick up her Sunday paper. I wave to her, and she waves back.

How could May even think that about me? I treated her really well with the dinner and flowers and stuff. I made sure she had a good time last night too. Twice.

I level Evie with a hard look. "Fine. I'll take a paternity test." *Even though I never slept with you.*

She waves airily. "That's not necessary. I know it was you."

May slams her car door and peels away.

"She seems upset," Evie says.

"You think?"

May

Some first date. A pregnant woman shows up, and Mason just tries to get rid of her. Who does that? He's not the man I thought he was. I dash at a tear. The man doesn't deserve my tears. This was supposed to be casual. I shouldn't care so much.

I look to the ceiling, blinking back tears. Then I start cleaning like a madwoman. I need to get the house ready for a party that happens in less than three hours.

My phone rings. Mason again. I send it to voicemail. There's nothing to talk about. We had one night of great sex. That's all.

I gather old magazines and school papers from the end table and shove them in the coffee table drawer. The door doesn't shut right away. I smack it into place. So what if last night was phenomenal? He was sweet, attentive, and generous in and out of bed. He got me flowers, chocolate, and wine. My three favorite things. And great sex, company, and food. I started thinking maybe we could meet up casually again.

I turn and arrange the throw pillows on the sofa. I punch a pillow. And then this pregnant woman shows up, and he doesn't even care!

How could I have been so wrong about him? And why do I care so much? It's not like we had a future.

I need coffee. I barely slept last night. My body heats at the memory. No. That's over.

I guzzle down a cup of coffee and get the vacuum cleaner out. A text chimes on my phone. Mason: *Can we talk?*

I ignore it. I saw his true colors this morning. It just makes it that much easier to let him go.

Sophie gets home and goes straight to her room to pick out her birthday party outfit. I pour myself a second cup of coffee, guzzle it down, and get back to work.

Finally, the house is clean and decorated for Sophie's party. There. I've done my part. I collapse on the sofa.

Sophie runs downstairs and joins me. "Thank you, Mommy. Everything looks so pretty."

I pull her close and kiss the top of her head. "You're welcome." I put up pink and purple streamers along with pink, purple, and white balloons I blew up myself. Probably should've sprung for the already inflated balloons at the party store. At least all that deep breathing calmed me down.

The doorbell rings, and I plaster on a smile, prepared to meet the party guests.

Sophie looks through the front window. "It's Mason! He came!"

I answer the door, smile frozen in place. "Hi, Mason. You're the first one here."

"Mason!" Sophie hugs his leg. "Thank you for the present."

"Happy birthday." He hands her a gift, and she runs to put it on the gift table.

"May, that woman this morning just wanted money," Mason says in a low voice.

I hold up a palm. "No need to explain." *Of course she wants money for the baby.*

My focus firmly on Sophie, I have her help me retrieve the party-favor bags from our apartment on the third floor. I can feel his eyes boring into me as I go upstairs. He doesn't owe me any explanation. It's over.

～

Mason

I stand near the edge of the room as little girls run through the downstairs. Their excited voices reach levels only dogs can hear. Not the time to talk to May about what happened this morning. But I'm not leaving here today until we can talk.

Another high-pitched shriek rings through the air. My shoulders tense, and I'm tempted to cover my ears, but just then Sophie runs by me and says, "I'm having the best time!"

I can't be a downer to the birthday girl. They've been playing an elaborate game of Twinkle Fairies led by Sophie. All the girls have fairy wings on their backs. Apparently, they were told to bring their wings from home.

"Where's your fairy wings?" Alice asks me with a grin.

"Guess I left them home. Didn't want to outshine the girls. They're huge."

"So I heard."

I do a double take at the innuendo. Did May tell Alice about last night? I thought it was just between us. Did she tell her about Evie showing up at my door too? No, she couldn't have. Alice is smiling way too much for that.

"She's glowing," Alice says. "Just look at her."

I find May in the center of the insanity, gently guiding girls off the furniture left and right. I'm tempted to yell that they heard the no-jumping-on-the-furniture rule when they got here, but it's not my place. It occurs to me that's what my parents would've done. Dad was in the military, and Mom was tough, so I'm used to a different parenting style.

"She just looks stressed," I tell Alice.

Alice shakes her head. "I know she went to your place for dinner, and she asked me to keep Sophie for the night. Good on you. She hasn't been with anyone in a year. Can you imagine?"

I catch May's eye. She frowns and looks away.

"Uh-oh, trouble in paradise already?" Alice asks.

May smiles sweetly at a little girl with a lopsided ponytail and guides her off the coffee table.

I have no answer for Alice, so I make myself useful, throwing sofa cushions on the floor. "The floor is lava."

The girls start hopping from cushion to cushion. I toss the cushions from the other sofa and some throw pillows for good measure.

May joins me, standing behind the sofa, and gives me a wry smile. "I should've thought of that."

The noise level quickly rises again as the girls shout at each other to avoid the lava.

May leans close to my ear. "I did warn you about six-year-old birthday parties. Do you have a headache?"

"No, but I'm pretty sure I lost part of my hearing." At least we're talking again. I thought she might manage to avoid me for the entire party. Someone's staring at me. Alice and her mom, Liz, watch us from across the room. Liz has a hopeful look on her face.

I whisper in May's ear, "It seems Alice and your mom know about last night."

"Shhh. Not in front of the..." She looks around. "Where is the birthday girl?"

"I found them!" Sophie announces, running into the room with a potato chip bag. She rips it open, and chips fly everywhere. The girls rush over to examine the mess.

"They're dirty," one girl says.

"They fell in the lava," another girl says.

"I don't mind lava," another girl says, picking up a chip and eating it.

"Ewww," the girls say at once. They walk as a group to the far side of the room, stomping some chips into the rug as they go.

Sophie stands there with a wobbly lower lip, clutching the ripped chip bag.

May rushes over to her. "It's okay. I'll clean it up." She dashes into the kitchen.

Sophie stares at the mess in horror. May appears with a garbage bag and makes quick work of cleanup.

"Now there's no more chips," Sophie says in a small voice.

"That was my favorite kind that we only get on special occasions, and now it's ruined." Her voice cracks.

Shit. She's going to cry at her own birthday party. I bolt into action, taking the bag from her hands. "I'll get another bag of chips just like this one." I pull my phone from my back pocket and take a picture of it. May holds out the garbage bag, and I drop the chip bag in. "No reason to cry now, okay? I'll be back before you can say pin the tail on the unicorn."

"Pin the tail on the unicorn," she says, still sounding teary.

"Let's play that game," May says, holding the garbage bag behind her back. Liz swoops in to dispose of it. "Everyone to the dining room." She turns to me as the girls stampede out. "You didn't have to do that, but thank you."

"No problem."

She turns and follows the girls into the dining room. Alice starts vacuuming chip crumbs.

I head out the door, the silence such a relief that my shoulders relax. I wasn't sure why I was here since Sophie was so busy with her friends, but now I know. I'm the potato chip guy.

By the time I get back, the girls are eating pizza at the dining room table. Guess there's no potato chip emergency anymore. I kinda liked the idea of being the hero.

A unicorn taped to a wall has rainbow tails all over it. Looks like I missed a lot. There was a crowd at the store, and I couldn't find the right brand at first. I went up and down the aisle several times before finding it on an endcap in the next aisle. Seems there was a sale.

I hand the bag of chips to May.

She smiles. "Thanks. After this is karaoke, cake, and party favors; then you can go."

"I still want to talk to you."

She shakes her head. "Not necessary." She holds up the potato chip bag. "Who wants chips?"

"ME-E-E-EE!" the girls say in near unison.

My head throbs from the noise. I look around for Liz and Alice, but they're not here. I walk out to the living room, where Liz is cleaning up and Alice is lying on the sofa with a washcloth over her forehead.

"Can I help?" I ask Liz.

Liz shoos me away. "You're a party guest. Go join the party."

"But it's so loud in there."

She laughs. "That's why Alice is battling a migraine."

"The things I do for my niece," Alice says. "I'll hold out for cake, but then I need to get to a dark quiet room."

"May will understand if you need to go," Liz says. "You can celebrate with Sophie at the family party."

"I took some medicine," Alice says. "I think I can make it to cake."

Hmmm, there's a family party, but Sophie wanted me here at her friend party. Why? I'm so out of place, and I feel like a lurking giant. Not that I want to go to a family party pretending May and I are just friends. If we're even that anymore. Besides, meeting her family is like inviting a woman to a wedding. Oh, wait. I already did that.

"You must really like May to endure six-year-old madness," Liz says, looking at me expectantly.

"We're friends," I say noncommittally.

"Ha!" Alice says, and then, "Ow, my head."

Liz pats my shoulder and puts the vacuum away. Back to the party and then, when all the guests leave, May and I will finally clear the air.

∽

May

Mason looked like a deer caught in the headlights for most of the party. I did warn him. It's kinda sweet that he made the effort to show up for Sophie. Also sweet that he rushed in to save the chips for her. Just because he has a sweet side doesn't mean I forgive him for treating that poor pregnant woman so callously. He was my first and last one-night stand. Probably not his first or last. Obviously, we could never be compatible.

Okay, yes, I initiated having a night alone with him, and it was great, but that's the end of it. In the harsh light of day, the reality is I'm better off without him.

He catches my eye and points his fork at the cake. "Did you make this?"

I nod. It's a three-layer chocolate cake with chocolate mousse in between the layers, topped with fudge icing.

"Amazing," he says, digging back in.

I help myself to a slice of cake, watching Sophie enjoy her day. I might be tired and cranky about Mason, but seeing Sophie so happy makes me feel good. She's enjoying her party with her friends.

"If you're done eating, raise your hand," Sophie says.

One by one the girls raise their hands, though some of them aren't done.

"Time for opening presents!" Sophie exclaims. She pushes back her chair and rushes from the room. I follow, keeping an eye on things. The girls gather in a circle on the floor of the living room while Sophie grabs a present from the gift table and sits with them to open it.

Mason's voice sounds near my ear, startling me. I didn't hear him approach with the girls' noise. "You're a good mom. So patient. You never yell."

"I've yelled before. I just have to be pushed enough to get there. Like yesterday when she decided to take a joyride in your pink Cadillac."

Our eyes meet, and we laugh. My heart kicks harder. No. I refuse to fall for this man.

"How much is the Cadillac worth?" I ask, thinking of Sophie damaging it.

He names a number so outlandish I can't find my voice for a moment. I never could've paid him back if there was damage. All I thought about was making sure Sophie was safe. That car has great value for his business.

"Guess you won't be inviting us back to the shop," I say.

"She won't do it again. She learned her lesson."

He says that so confidently it makes me want to laugh. "Did she, really?"

"I hope so."

The doorbell rings. Alice lets them in.

"Olivia H.'s mom's here," I announce.

Olivia H. throws her head back in anguish. "Why do I have to be first? Please can I stay longer, Mommy?"

Olivia H.'s mom, Cara, is the alpha of the parent-teacher association at Clover Park elementary school. Her honey-blond hair is perfectly highlighted and falls in soft layers around her perfectly made-up face. "We need to get going. Tell Sophie and her mom thank you." Her eye catches on Mason, and she gives him an appreciative once-over. See? He's handsome and sexy to all women not just me. That's why he's on TV.

Cara lifts her brows at me in question.

I shrug one shoulder. She knows Mason's not there for my mom or sister. They're both married. This is going to make a splash with the mom grapevine.

Mom gives Olivia H. a party-favor bag full of quiet toys—a top, bubbles, and fairy stickers. I wouldn't be so evil as to send them home with candy and whistles, which another mom did at a preschool birthday party we went to last year. All I can say is nightmare car ride home with my sugar-addled kid. Though not as bad as the Lecture and Sex Talk ride home we enjoyed yesterday. My Lord, I sweated through that one.

"Thank you, Mrs. Herman," Olivia H. says sweetly.

"You're welcome. Thank you for coming. Sophie!" My daughter hasn't stopped opening presents.

Sophie waves. "Bye, Olivia H.! Thank you for the present, even though I haven't opened it yet."

"I'll come over tomorrow to play with—"

"Don't tell her; it's a surprise," Cara says.

Olivia H. jumps up and down. "Ooh, Sophie, you'll love it. I want one too so bad."

Sophie smiles and waves. They leave, and I spy Alice on the porch swing. I cross my arms against the cold. "Aren't you freezing?"

"I feel better out here. I'll greet people as they come and let them in, okay?"

I go inside, grab her coat from the hook, and hand it to her. "Go home. I can answer the door."

She puts her arms in the sleeves. "Have Mason open the door. All the moms could use some eye candy."

"Ha-ha."

"I'm serious."

"I'm sure he wants to leave too." I lower my voice to a whisper. "I'm shocked he showed up. We didn't leave things on good terms this morning, and a six-year-old's birthday party isn't exactly his scene."

"You're fighting already? What about?"

"It was a onetime thing, and I don't need the drama." I give her a push. "Go. Feel better. And thank you for all your help."

She waves and hurries to her car. I'm thankful I don't get migraines from too much noise. Otherwise, how could I ever manage Sophie and what I hope will be a busy inn?

Parents start showing up, and I greet them, ready for their kids to leave. I need a quiet room and a glass of wine. I have a feeling Sophie will crash after all this excitement. Maybe we can both take naps.

Mason jumps in to help, handing out goody bags as the girls leave. Wow, he's really hanging in there until the end.

"You don't need to stay," I say after another mom and kid leaves.

"I want to talk to you, so I'll hang in a bit longer."

"Nothing to talk about."

"Yes, there is."

A group of parents arrive. Mason works with me through a flurry of goodbyes, helping to get jackets on and hand out goody bags. If anyone's wondering who he is, they haven't said anything.

Finally, the last girl leaves.

Sophie twirls her long light brown hair, a sign she's tired. "That was a great party, Mommy. Can I watch TV?"

"Yes." I decided punishing her by taking away TV time would be hard on me too, so instead she doesn't get dessert for a month. Except her birthday. I know, I'm a softie.

Once I hear the TV turn on, I turn to Mason. "What do you want to talk about?"

He clears his throat, draws me close and speaks directly in my ear. Hot shivers race down my spine at the low rumble of his voice. "The woman who showed up this morning, Evie, just wanted to be on the show. I never slept with her. We met briefly at Happy Endings. That's it."

"So she's not pregnant?" I whisper.

He pulls back to look at me. "No."

"You seemed so uncaring."

"Because I knew it wasn't true. She went from pregnant and wanting child support to wanting to be on the show to asking for a thousand dollars to cover her rent in exchange for sex."

My jaw drops.

He pushes my chin up, closing my mouth. "You don't know me well enough to know this, but I don't hook up with random women."

I look into his eyes and see only sincerity. Now I'm embarrassed I thought the worst of him. "I guess you just wait for them to invite themselves over for dinner."

He grins. "I had a good time last night."

"Me too."

He leans close, his lips brushing my cheek. "Do you want to see me again?" His voice is a whisper with a note of hope.

I smile. "Yes."

He smiles too, his eyes trailing to my cheek, my lips, and back to my eyes. He leans close to my ear again. "Your friends saw me here, your mom and sister know we were together last night, so can we go out in public together? Or is this strictly an inside-the-house thing?"

I read between the lines. Relationship or casual sex?

I whisper back, "Inside the house in complete secret is best. The important thing is Sophie's kept out of it. I don't want people talking. Word gets around fast in a small town."

He nods solemnly.

"If you're okay with that," I say. "I understand if you're at a place in your life when maybe you're looking for more, and if that's the case, by all means, go out there and find it."

The corner of his mouth lifts in an adorable lopsided smile. "You know, it's crazy, even after surviving a girl rager, I still want you." His eyes smolder into mine, and suddenly I want him, too, like right now.

"Can I have a juice box?" Sophie asks, running to the kitchen. She doesn't even look at us.

"Yes!" I say.

She runs back to the family room.

Mason leans in for a kiss, but I push him away. "Thanks for coming!"

He grins. "Thank you for coming too."

I flush and shake my head. "Bye."

"When can I see you again?"

"I'll text you."

He gazes at me with such longing it hits me that it's more than lust for him. He likes me too. "Okay," he says, and then louder, "Bye, Sophie! Happy birthday!"

"Bye! I can't get the straw in the juice box."

Mason goes to help her, but I put a hand on his arm, stopping him. "My job."

"Right."

I go to help Sophie and hear the front door shut. Did I do the right thing agreeing to see him again? For how long can I keep this a secret casual thing? I'm playing a dangerous game. Who am I kidding? I'm already falling. Who wouldn't after he was so generous with his repairs and naked time and coming to my daughter's birthday party.

I join Sophie on the sofa and put an arm around her. She leans into my side and looks up at me. "Are you and Mason getting married?"

I freeze. "Why would you ask that?"

"All my friends say you are. Can I pick out the cake for the wedding?" She knows all about weddings now, but she doesn't get adult relationships.

Damn, she's already too invested. "No, sweetheart, we're not getting married. He's just a nice man who fixes things, and we return the favor by making him dinner. Adults can be complicated."

"It's simple, Mommy. You like each other, fall in love, and get married."

"We're not doing that. Mason and I are friends like you and Olivia H. are friends. He's very busy and so am I. We probably won't have time to see each other much."

"That sucks."

"Sophie! Don't say sucks. It's rude."

She lets out a big sigh. "I guess I wasted my birthday wish."

Her birthday wish was for me and Mason to get married?!

"Watch your show. I'm going to make popcorn."

"Okay!"

I go in the kitchen and get a bag of microwave popcorn and put it in the microwave. While that cooks, I text Mason.

Me: *Sophie thinks we're getting married. I'm not sure this is going to work between us, even casually.*

Mason: *Can't you just say we're friends?*

I don't reply because I'm not sure what to say. I turn the ringer off on my phone in case he calls. I rub my temple. I do have feelings for him. I'm on a tightrope between potential love in my life and protecting my daughter. What an impossible choice.

The microwave dings. I put the popcorn in a bowl and grab some napkins, heading back to the family room.

Sophie's on the sofa with shreds of wrapping paper around her. "Look what Mason got me!"

She holds up a black T-shirt that says *Hot Finds* with flames around the letters. Then she shows me a pink Cadillac toy car that looks just like the one she admired and drove.

I steel myself against all the mushy feelings welling up for a man who somehow managed to find a pink Cadillac in the four hours between when I ran out of his house and getting ready for a party. All for my little girl. He cares about her.

But would he be a part of our life long term? I'm a package deal I'm not sure he's ready for, and it's not fair of me to ask that of him.

10

I lasted a week without Mason. Days of trying not to think about him. Nights of vivid, sexy dreams. I only caved because it's raining inside my house. On a Saturday, of course, when plumbers cost extra. I called a plumber, but it'll take time for him to finish with his other emergency job before he can get here. My parents are away with my uncles and aunts for a winter break in Bermuda. Mason will know what to do. He'll be here any minute.

Here's how the disaster happened—while I was showering in our apartment on the top floor, Sophie took a shower in one of the guest bathrooms without my permission to "try it out." The shower liner was outside the tub, which was basically like showering in the open. Water pooled on the floor and under the baseboard to the ceiling downstairs. It was a *long* shower.

Even if she did leave the liner out, it seems it should've made a puddle on the floor not flooded the ceiling. I've got towels down on the foyer floor, and the ceiling has a large bubble, which will likely pop, leaving an unsightly hole.

I stare at the bubble, willing it to stop dripping. Sophie's lying on her stomach on the living room rug with her connect-the-dots book. We had a long talk about how shower curtains work. Her reply, "Okay. Make sure to tell your guests that, or we'll have the same problem all over again." Like everyone is confused about how shower curtains work. Ha.

I hear a truck and peek out the window. Mason. I smooth my hair, my heart kicking harder. I don't know why I'm excited. We're not seeing each other anymore. And there's nothing sexy about a plumbing emergency.

I open the door before he can ring the bell. "Thanks so much for coming. I didn't know who else to call." I wince because it sounds like I didn't want to call him when it's perfectly fine to be acquaintances who see each other sometimes. "I called the plumber, but he couldn't get here quick on a Saturday because of another job."

He steps inside and looks at the ceiling, all business. "What happened?"

"Hi, Mason!" Sophie says cheerfully. "I'm connecting the dots, and then I'm going to color the picture."

"Cool," he says. He turns to me in question.

I tell him the shower story and gesture for him to follow me upstairs. When we get to the bathroom, he looks at the shower and tub and crouches down to look at the floor.

He stands. "You'll need to add a corner lip over here because it's too easy for water to spill out on this side. They should have what you need at the hardware store." Does he think I know what that is and how to install it?

"Uh, do you think you could find a corner lip and install it? I'll reimburse you for the cost."

He shoves his hands in his jeans' pockets. "Sure."

"Good because I don't even know what a corner lip is." I smile. He doesn't smile back.

Guess he's not cool with being acquaintances. Maybe he's mad I called him?

"Should I not have called you? I didn't know who else to call. My parents are on vacation with—"

"It's fine." He doesn't sound like it's fine.

I lead the way out. On the way downstairs, he says, "I'll fix the drywall on the ceiling too. Just need to let it dry out for a week. Fixable. Got a bucket?"

"Yeah, I'll get it."

When I return with the bucket, he takes out a multi-use pocketknife and makes a small cut in the bubble. Dad would approve. He always says everyone should carry a multi-use pocketknife because you never know. I keep that to myself.

Water drips into the bucket. Not a flood like I thought. Maybe this isn't so bad.

"You don't need a plumber," Mason says. "What you need is a better constructed floor that's sealed in the bathroom, but unless you want to demo the bathroom and renovate again, I think the corner lip on the tub should do the trick."

Sophie looks up from the floor at Mason. "Are you going to fix it?"

"Yup. Just need to get a few items from the hardware store for the tub. It'll take three days to repair the drywall on the ceiling. I'll come back in a week for that."

Sophie sits up. "Mommy, are you going to pay him with dinner again?"

"Uh…"

Mason holds up a palm. "Not necessary. Alright, I'll be back in a bit."

He leaves.

I close the door behind him and lean against it. He's respecting the line I drew, no warm smiles, no flirting. It's much worse than a clean break because I miss his warm smiles.

I'm so confused.

The next day after dinner, the doorbell rings. It can't be Mason. He said he'd be back in a week for the ceiling repair, and he already added that lip thingy to the tub.

I peek through the peephole. It's a woman with a short bob of brown hair, wearing a silver puffy coat. *Oh shit. It's Mason's mom. What's she doing here?*

I open the door. "Hi, is everything okay?"

Her expression is fierce. "Not really. Remember me from the wedding?" I back up as she advances, letting herself in.

"Of course, you're Mason's mom. Is he okay?"

"He's fine." She looks up at the damaged ceiling. "You got a water leak."

"Yes. It'll be fixed in a week."

"Mason again."

"Mrs. Shaw—"

"Madison."

"Madison, Mason has been a huge help to me. I'm sure you can imagine how costly it is to turn an old house into an inn. And then all these extra repairs keep popping up. I want to open on Valentine's Day, which is only four weeks away." I put a hand to my forehead, suddenly overwhelmed. "I have so much work to do. I didn't even start getting the word out. I've been so busy trying to get everything set up."

She puts a palm up. "I don't care about any of that. I'm here about Mason. This situation isn't going to work. He's not ready for…" She trails off as Sophie runs in wearing a dress, pants, fairy wings and a fireman's helmet.

She stops short in front of Madison. "Who are you?"

"Who are you?" Madison returns.

"I'm Sophie Herman."

"Sophie, this is Mason's mom, Mrs. Shaw. You met her briefly at the wedding."

"I can do a cartwheel, wanna see?"

She then proceeds to cartwheel, somersault, and attempt a handstand before I rescue her from hitting the end table. She pushes the hair out of her face. "Ta-dah!"

"Nice work," Madison says. "You should clear the furniture before you do gymnastics."

Sophie starts pushing the coffee table out of the way.

"No more gymnastics," I say.

Sophie jumps on the sofa and bounces a little so her wings flap. "I wish I could fly."

Madison's expression softens. "I heard Mason went to your birthday party."

Sophie leaps off the sofa. "Yup. He's going to be my daddy."

Madison sucks in air.

Sophie continues blithely, "It just takes time and a spark for people to get married, which is how you turn into a daddy. That's what Aunt Alice says."

I leap in. "No, sweetheart. Mason and I aren't getting married."

"Then how can he be my daddy?" Sophie turns to Madison. "I asked for a daddy for Christmas, and Santa didn't bring him, then on my birthday candle secret wish, I thought let Mason be my daddy real hard, and it didn't come true."

Madison gives me a significant look. I shake my head.

Sophie continues, "I hope the Easter Bunny will make it come true. I'm going to write him a letter like we did for Santa, but instead of Dear Santa, it'll say Dear Easter Bunny. Then we just need a spark so we can have the wedding. Mommy, the spark's your job."

"Sophie, wishes won't make a new daddy appear," I say gently.

"Everyone in my class has a daddy!" Sophie cries. "Tate has two daddies, and I have none. It's not fair." She stomps upstairs.

Madison watches her go. "She's got spirit. That's good. It'll keep her strong."

I laugh a little. "That's one way to put it."

Madison smiles, making her seem almost approachable. "She reminds me a little of myself at that age. Strong, opinionated, showing off for attention. Only instead of a dad, I wanted a mom desperately. Mine left when I was one. I remember how badly I wanted a mom like the other kids in my class. Not the one who left. A new, better one."

"I'm sure that was very difficult."

She narrows her brown eyes at me. "You have no idea what you're doing, do you?"

"What do you mean?"

"Dating as a single mom."

"Mason and I are just friends. In fact, I'm not going to date anyone until Sophie's in college."

She gives me a skeptical look. "You're sending him mixed messages. Asking him to fix things, inviting him to dinner. He raves about your cooking." She lowers her voice. "My son has never been to a six-year-old girl's birthday party. Not since he was six. You think he would do all that for a friend? I know he stays late here. My nieces told me."

My cheeks heat. "That part's over now. I ended it."

She continues as if I haven't spoken. "I came here to warn you away from Mason. And I say this for your benefit. He's not ready to be a dad. His ex-girlfriend had a pregnancy scare six months ago, and he *freaked out*. He's not even sure if he ever wants to get married. None of my boys are." Her brows scrunch together. "Which doesn't make sense since their dad and I have a happy marriage. Maybe the boys are too busy sowing their wild oats. Anyway, you might not *think* you're doing anything, but you're reeling him in."

Like I'm some master seductress. Right. Fix my plumbing! Wait, that sounds bad.

"I think you need to leave now," I say, walking to the door.

"Hire a repairman. I'll send you some recommendations. I work in real estate. I know everyone, which I imagine would be important to someone opening an inn. I could be a real help to you."

I open the door. "I'll be sure to tell Mason you were here."

"Oh, no need for that. Really. Good luck with the inn!" She dashes out the door.

I shut the door and lean back against it with a sigh. Suddenly I realize it's awfully quiet upstairs. Quiet's never good where Sophie's concerned. I take the stairs at a run.

~

Mason

My jaw drops. "You did what?" I'm on the phone with Mom, who crossed the line big time.

"I had a talk with her, woman to woman," Mom says. "It had to be done."

"No, it *didn't* have to be done."

"Sophie wants a dad like I always wanted a mom."

"Which is why May cut me loose. I can't believe you went to her house. Too far!"

"First a wedding, then a six-year-old's birthday party, and your cousins say you're there a lot for dinner and repairing stuff for her. What am I supposed to think? She's reeling you in, and you don't even know it. You're not ready for that scene. Remember when Christina thought she was pregnant? You were in panic mode."

"Because I was about to end it when that happened. I didn't want to be tied to Christina for the rest of my life." I exhale sharply. "You didn't have to go over there. What did she say when you talked to her? Was she surprised to see you?"

"I imagine she was surprised. She said she ended it, and if you'd told me that, none of this would've happened."

"Don't put this on me."

"I'm sorry. I was worried. And when I heard Sophie talk about how much she wanted a daddy, I knew that feeling. It's hard to bear that absence in your life."

Mom's mom bailed on her when she was one; Dad's mom died young from a drug overdose. Somewhere deep inside, Mom still has a little girl who wants a mother.

"Mason, Sophie's birthday wish was for you to be her daddy. Only move forward with May if you're going to commit. I mean *married* commit. Otherwise, it's not fair to either of them."

I still. That's a big deal for a kid to use her birthday wish on me. If Sophie never knew about us, I would steal every moment I could with May. But Sophie does know, and now her hopes are tied to me.

"I get it," I say. "I won't be seeing May again anyway."
Except for the repairs next week.

"I like Sophie. She reminds me of myself at that age. High energy, impulsive, loud."

"But sweet, too, unlike you."

"All little kids are sweet. She'll grow out of that, and that's not a bad thing."

May's sweet too. Fun and kind and sexy. I keep that to myself. I can think whatever I want about May as long as I don't act on it.

"I'm hanging up now," I say.

"Bye."

I stand there for a moment, thinking about May. She cut things off before we got in deep enough to even consider a future. I guess with a single mom you always need to consider the future.

Am I ready to be a family man? That always seemed like something for older, settled-down guys. A daughter? I don't know how to do girl hair or girl talk or girl clothes. Fairies and stuffed animal collections are foreign territory to me. Though I see the appeal of Hornbow the unicorn. She can fly and do magic.

No. I enjoy my freedom. I come and go as I please, answer to no one (except my nosy family), and make as much of a mess as I feel like at home.

"Bachelor life for me," I say to the quiet house.

I flop on the sofa, grab the remote, and turn on the game to fill the silence.

11

———

May

Not long after Mason's mom visited, I was surprised to get an email from Shayla and Owen's wedding photographer, Rafael, asking if I could have the inn ready in a week for a photo session for the website and marketing materials. I did everything I could to get it in tiptop shape, besides the ceiling repair. Mason must've sent him. He didn't have to do that. I can't help but feel warmly toward a man who goes out of his way to help me, asking nothing in return.

All week I had hope in my heart. Even though I pushed Mason away, he's still in my life. That means something. He cares about me as a person not just a casual fling.

I was hoping to see him today, but a man named Ralph showed up in Mason's place this morning to repair the ceiling. I guess he's keeping his distance. I had made Mason a dinner to take with him as a thank you for the repair work, since I know he likes my cooking, and gave it to Ralph instead. Ralph's in his sixties and divorced. He was thrilled with a home-cooked meal since he eats frozen dinners every night.

I hate to admit it, but when I saw Ralph this morning, all the hope leaked out of me. Mason cares, yes, but he doesn't want to see me. That hurt more than it should have considering I'm the one who ended it. Maybe I made a mistake.

After Ralph leaves, Sophie asks, "When's Mason coming over again?"

"I don't know. He's really busy. Hey, how about we invite Olivia H. or Carrie over for a playdate after the photo session?"

"Can they both come?"

"Sure. I'll text their moms."

"Yay!" She runs toward the kitchen. "I'm thirsty!"

The doorbell rings. That must be the photographer.

I open the door to a tall, handsome guy with short brown hair, sparkling blue eyes, and a scruffy jaw. He could be a model or a movie star. Movie star, definitely. "Hi, Rafael." I didn't notice how strikingly handsome he is at the wedding. Probably because my focus was on Mason.

He flashes a smile that lights up his face. "Hey, nice to see you again. Not sure if I mentioned before, I'm the groom's younger brother." I connect the dots. Mason's cousin and Claire Jordan's son. No wonder he's movie-star handsome.

"I see the resemblance now. Come in."

He steps inside. "Mason covered my fee, so don't give it another thought."

"He did?"

"Yup."

"I'll have to return the favor somehow."

"Nah, just let him do his gallant thing." He winks.

I laugh. "Come on. I'll show you everything I want to highlight. The third floor is my apartment, so we can skip that."

"Sure."

Sophie appears from the kitchen, wearing a milk mustache. "Who are you?"

"Rafael," he says. "And you're Sophie."

Her eyes widen. "How do you know my name?"

"We met at the wedding, but I was mostly behind a

camera." He holds the camera to his face and then lowers it. "I'm taking pictures of the inn for your mom today."

"How long do I have to wait for my playdate?" Sophie asks me.

"I'll see if you can go to their house. Go get ready while I check on who's around."

She runs upstairs.

"I'll send you digital proofs tonight," Rafael says. "You can pick your favorites. I'll do some editing and send you the finals."

"Thanks so much."

"I'll take pictures of the house first, and then I'd like to get some of you on the front porch."

"Absolutely." He starts with the living room, and I dash upstairs to change into something nicer than a baggy sweater and leggings. It was so sweet of Mason to do this for me.

What does it mean?

~

The next morning, a young brunette woman shows up at my door, holding a binder. Another guest I remember from the wedding. She's engaged to Cooper Campbell, Mason's cousin.

She smiles and holds out her hand. "Hi, I'm Rowan Sanders. We met briefly at Shayla and Owen's wedding. I'm a partner in Love Junkies, the premier wedding planning service in town."

"Yes, I remember you. You and Cooper looked so happy together on the dance floor."

She smiles. "We're very happy. Anyway, I'm here to help you with marketing and social media campaigns for the inn. It's my specialty at Love Junkies, and I used to run my own ad agency." She holds up her binder. "I've got lots of ideas, but of course I'd love to hear yours too."

I'm floored. First Rafael takes professional photos, and

now a marketing expert is here to help me with the over-whelming task of getting the word out for the inn.

I step back. "Please come in. I'm so happy to have someone to bounce ideas off of, and I'd love to hear yours. What's your rate?"

She waves that away. "All taken care of."

"By Mason?"

"It's what our family does. We help each other out. You're important to Mason, so that means you're in."

"But I'm not family. Mason and I aren't even together anymore."

She pats my arm. "Mmm-hmm. It was weird for me at first too. You'll get used to it."

Is this Mason making a grand gesture?

Rowan looks at me expectantly, and I snap into action. "I'll give you the tour, and then we can get to work at the kitchen table." Fortunately, Sophie's out for Sunday brunch with my parents. They're back from Bermuda.

"Sounds like a plan!" She sets her binder down on the coffee table and pulls her phone from her purse. "I'll take notes as I go."

As I take her on the tour, she stops frequently, taking in the view from various windows and sitting on furniture as she dictates into her phone. She's very thorough.

All I can think is that if Mason keeps sending people to help me, it must mean he's serious about me. And that means maybe, just maybe, I can take a risk and let him in. WWMD? Grandmom Maggie was all about taking risks in life. She always said you can hide under your bed, but then the bed could collapse on you.

But it's not just a risk for me. There's Sophie too. If I'm careful to protect Sophie from high expectations, maybe this could work.

∾

After Rowan leaves, my head's spinning. I had no idea social media could have such complex ways of spreading word of mouth. We worked out a budget for advertising, and she said she'll be sure to recommend the inn to her wedding clients. I agreed to recommend Love Junkies to any engaged couples who stay here, so it's a win-win.

I have to thank Mason for all his help. My parents took Sophie to the movies after brunch, so I've still got a couple of hours before she gets home. I grab my coat and purse and head out the door.

A short while later, I arrive at his house and ring the bell.

He answers the door, his brows shooting up. "May, is everything okay?"

"Yes. I just stopped by to thank you for sending over Rafael and Rowan to help with the inn's launch. They were both so helpful. I really appreciate it."

He steps back, gesturing for me to come inside.

I shove my hands in my coat pockets, suddenly awkward. I remember every detail of our dinner here and our night together.

One corner of his mouth turns up. "It was my way of apologizing for my buttinsky mom going to your house and warning you away. Sorry about that. She's never done that before to someone I'm seeing. It was completely unnecessary anyway, right?"

My shoulders droop. "Right. I mean, I did say we shouldn't see each other anymore."

"Which I completely understand. Sophie is your number one priority."

I swallow hard. "I think I messed up."

"With what?"

I meet his eyes. "I like you a lot."

He steps closer, his voice turning husky. "I like you a lot too."

"And-and I think I'm ready for more. With you."

He tucks a lock of hair behind my ear. "May, I'm honored. But what about Sophie? She seemed to be onto us from the start. I'd like to see where things go with us without Sophie thinking I'm stepping in as her dad."

"We could just tell her we're going out as friends?"

He quirks a brow. "That's not going to fool her."

"Okay, well, then I don't know what to do. I don't want her heart to break if things don't work out."

"Or yours."

"Or mine," I admit.

He pulls me into his arms. "Would it help if I told you I missed you fiercely and can't stop thinking about you?"

I wrap my arms around his neck, reveling in the heat and strength of his body pressed close. "It would. Me too. I'm scared of all I'm feeling."

His eyes soften. "Me too. I've never felt this way before."

My heart cracks open. "Oh, Mason."

"This doesn't come along every day."

My eyes well. I had love once, and I've been afraid to let myself love again. "I know."

"We can take it slow. Just the two of us, okay? We'll leave our families out of it. You've already seen how nosy my family is, and until you feel comfortable having me around Sophie, I'll stay away. I understand why that's necessary, but, May, I need to see you. I'm falling in love with you."

He cradles my face and kisses me tenderly, reverently. My heart soars. This is right. I have to take a chance on love again.

I drop off Sophie at my parents' house for a sleepover the following weekend. I told her I'm spending time with some old college friends this weekend. I don't like to lie, but it was the only way I could think of to keep her from hoping for something that may not happen.

I set her backpack inside the living room. She runs to hug Mom.

Mom strokes her hair. "We're going to have so much fun

at our sleepover. Tonight we'll watch a movie with popcorn, and tomorrow we'll go sledding. The snow on the hill behind the elementary school is perfect."

"What movie?" Sophie asks.

"A little birdie told me you've been wanting to see *Hoppity*." That's an Easter Bunny movie that came out last year. Sophie's been looking forward to Easter a lot this year, even though it's two months away. I guess she's old enough to really appreciate fun holiday traditions.

"Yes!"

Sophie runs over to Dad and throws herself at his legs. He picks her up, holding her upside down. She laughs madly as he carries her into the kitchen.

Mom studies my expression. "So things are going well with Mason?"

I bite back a smile, almost afraid to let myself feel happy. "It's early yet." We texted every day this week and talked for hours last night. I woke up this morning giddy about seeing him. I keep that to myself since Mason and I agreed to keep our nosy families out of it, but Mom knows all.

"You look happy. I think he's good for you."

"Let's not jump ahead. Like I said, it's all new. We're still getting to know each other."

"When do we get to have him over for dinner?"

"Not anytime soon."

"Have you met his parents?"

"Once at the wedding and once when his mom came to my house and told me he wasn't ready for the responsibility of a family, so I should back off. That was pleasant."

"Is that true? He's opposed to a family?"

"She said his ex had a pregnancy scare, and he freaked out, so I guess so. We agreed to take it slow."

She glances behind her. Dad and Sophie are still in the kitchen, probably getting hot cocoa. Dad's specialty. "You know I once had a pregnancy scare, and I freaked out, even though I love kids."

I stare at her, shocked. "Mom, you never told me that."

"It was with your dad before things were solid between us."

"Wow."

"A surprise pregnancy takes time to get used to. I wouldn't hold it against him for freaking out. Kids change your life forever. Well, you know that." She squeezes my arm. "A child that's planned for and very much wanted is a different story."

I blow out a breath. "Okay, I don't want to think about this right now. Tonight's just dinner." I kiss her cheek. "Bye, Mom. Thanks for watching her."

"She's my one and only grandchild. I'd have her over every day if I could, but I think you'd miss her too much. Have fun tonight and take your time getting her tomorrow. Sledding can take a while, and then there's hot cocoa."

Sophie appears in the living room, chewing on something. "Grandpop got the tiny marshmallows."

"Is there any other way to drink hot cocoa?" Mom asks.

Sophie shakes her head, smiling.

I walk over to Sophie and kiss the top of her head. "Have fun. I'll see you tomorrow."

"Bye, Mom. Have fun with your old friends."

Mom stifles a laugh.

"Thanks, Sophie. Be good."

"I'm always good." She hugs me. "I love you, Mommy."

My heart squeezes. "I love you too."

I leave with heavy feet. It's okay, I assure myself. I'm allowed to have dinner with a man. Sophie's having her special time with her grandparents tonight, and I'm having me time. *No guilt, no guilt, no guilt.*

Dinner is lovely. Mason took me to an upscale steakhouse in Fieldridge, not far from Clover Park. I had a filet mignon with red wine. Now we're having dessert. I got a chocolate soufflé. He got bread pudding.

"How's your dessert?" he asks.

"To die for."

"Good. Want to try mine?"

"No, thanks. I don't want to ruin the chocolate taste in my mouth."

"Fair enough." He takes a bite of his bread pudding, watching me enjoy my dessert. I should try making chocolate soufflé at home.

When we finish our desserts, Mason asks for the check and leans back in his seat. "What do you think about going away for a ski weekend next weekend? Aunt Claire has a cabin in Maine."

"Oh, um, a whole weekend?"

"We can ski or snowshoe, have a crackling fire. You'll love it."

"I don't want to leave Sophie for a whole weekend, plus the inn. I still don't have any bookings for Valentine's Day weekend. I'm afraid I got started too late on the marketing, but I was holding off until the inn was completely finished."

"I'm sure you'll have some last-minute husbands and boyfriends who book something. Have you seen the card section on Valentine's Day?"

"No, actually."

He slashes a hand through the air. "Filled with guys who waited until the last minute to get a card for Valentine's Day."

I hesitate. "I've always been close by on the weekend in case Sophie needs me."

He holds up a palm. "I get it."

"Sorry."

"I was just thinking how much fun we'd have up there. That's all." He signs the check and stands. "Ready?"

I sense a coolness in his tone, like he's not happy with the boundaries I set. "You and I can have fun around here next weekend, right? Or you could go with another friend to Maine. I don't mind."

"It's fine. We agreed to take it slow."

"I'm glad you understand."

He puts a hand on the small of my back and guides me out of the restaurant. When we get outside, he blows out a breath. "I'll drive you home."

"No! I mean, we don't need to take things *that* slow. I'm free all night for whatever."

He gives me a sexy smile, wrapping his arms around my waist. "I remember whatever being good between us."

"Whatever was better than good. It was phenomenal."

He nuzzles my neck, kissing his way up to my ear. He gives my earlobe a tug between his teeth. "Sweetest words I've ever heard." He caresses my cheek and gives me a tender kiss, gazing deep into my eyes.

Emotion clogs my throat, my heart thudding in my ears. I'm diving into the deep end. It's scary and exhilarating at the same time.

The moment we walk into Mason's house, we collide in a passionate kiss. His hands are all over me, and I'm loving it. This is exactly what I need.

He breaks the kiss, his eyes smoldering into mine. My lips part, my breath coming harder. And then he surprises me, scooping me up and carrying me upstairs.

"You really are gallant," I say once we're upstairs.

He pushes open the bedroom door and kicks it closed. "I like to think of it as romantic."

"Rafael says you sent him to my place to take pictures because you were gallant."

"That was me embarrassed that another person in my family, who will remain nameless, stopped by your house to talk about me."

I stroke his stubbled jaw. "Just us tonight."

"Just us."

He pulls back the covers and sets me gently in the center of the bed. I sit up and take off my top and bra.

His gaze heats. "May, you're so beautiful."

"Thank you. Now get naked."

Within moments, we're both naked. I open my arms to him. He covers me, kissing me urgently. The intensity ratches up instantly.

He lifts his head, gazing at me tenderly, then stroking down my throat. He kisses his way down my body. My limbs get heavy, and I sigh.

He kisses my stomach reverently. My worries over my stretch marks melt away. Mason makes me feel like a goddess.

He drops a kiss on my sex, making me jolt, before levering back up to kiss me on the lips.

He kisses the corner of my mouth, then the other corner, and when my lips part, he claims my mouth. The kiss goes on and on, and then something changes, and it turns harder, rougher, deeper.

He kisses his way down my body, arranging my legs over his shoulders. I throb in anticipation. He strokes me gently once, twice, and then his lips replace his fingers. My hips arch, seeking more of the amazing pleasure. Within moments, I'm rocking to his rhythm, climbing closer and closer to release. His fingers thrust inside me as his mouth works me, firm and hungry.

So close, so close. I'm beyond the power of speech, lost in sensation, and then I explode, wave after wave of pleasure firing through me. He stays with me, gentling as he wrings every last drop of pleasure from me until I'm spent. I close my eyes and throw my arms to my sides.

"You're so sexy," he growls. I hear the rustle of the condom wrapper, and then he's on me.

He kisses me, and I taste myself. Sexy. Intimate. He groans into my mouth as he guides himself inside me. I wrap my arms and legs around him, reveling in the deep connection.

He lifts his head, his dark eyes smoldering into mine as

he moves, a slow and steady rhythm that rocks me to my core. I feel so alive with pleasure and love, and it radiates back to me with every look and touch from this wonderful man.

I kiss him passionately. He breaks the kiss, his eyes glazed with lust as he takes me fast and hard, no more holding back. Our breaths mingle, both of us breathing harder as we go on this wild ride together. And then he hits just the right spot, making me gasp, his gaze the only thing keeping me grounded in the swirl of sensations. And then I go off, triggering his own release. I clutch his shoulders, overwhelmed with pleasure.

A few moments later, he kisses me tenderly and rolls to his back. His arm goes around me, pulling me close. I rest my cheek on his chest, listening to his wildly thumping heart.

Mason finally speaks, sounding like he just ran a marathon. "I love you."

My heart leaps.

"I know it's too soon, and you don't have to say it back."

I lift my head to look at him. "I love you too."

He kisses me tenderly.

I settle my head back on his chest and smile. "I have a feeling we're in for a wild ride together."

He kisses my temple. "That's the best kind."

The next morning, Mason makes us cheese omelets, and we sit at a small kitchen table in the corner. It's so cozy. Like our own little cocoon.

"Let me run something by you," Mason says.

I cut another piece of omelet. "Sure."

"Dad and I were brainstorming ideas for a promo for next season, and Dad thought it would be funny to have Sophie pretend to drive a Cadillac."

"You told him about that?"

"I kinda had to because we had to polish it up again.

Anyway, it wouldn't be the pink one, but we could get another Cadillac."

"I don't want to encourage her driving at this age."

"We'll tell her it's just pretend for TV. Like when you pretend to drive those little cars in a circle at the fair."

"I don't know."

"Just an idea."

"She *is* a fan of the show."

"As are you."

I smile. "Actually, I think at this point I can admit I was a fan of *you* not the show."

He puts a hand to his chest in mock surprise. "I'm shocked. I thought you were impressed by my car expertise."

I grab him by his T-shirt, pull him close, and kiss him.

He pulls back, straightening his shirt. "At least I know Sophie was in it for the cars. So what do you think about Sophie doing a promo?"

"I don't know. I need to think about it."

"Come on, it'll be fun. The car won't be moving. They'll add that with special effects. She'd just be sitting there pretending to steer and honk the horn."

"Okay, I'll mention it to her. If she wants to do it—"

"She's going to want to do it. Fan of the show, fan of Cadillacs, a chance to be on TV. They'll pay her too."

"I'll put the money in her college fund."

Our eyes meet, and we smile.

"Maybe use just a little of the money for fun?" he asks.

"Maybe."

"You're a tough mom."

"How many kids get to pretend-drive a Cadillac on TV? That's reward enough."

"Just one."

"Now back to our regularly scheduled programming." He takes my hand, guiding me up from my seat. His arms go around me as he nuzzles his way up my neck. Hot tingles race through me.

"What about breakfast?" I ask breathlessly.

He stops to look at me, perturbed. "If you're still asking about breakfast, I'm not doing this right."

He gives me a sexy smile before kissing me, backing me up toward the counter. He lifts me, pressing his body between my legs. I wrap my arms and legs around him, breakfast forgotten. I'm as hungry for Mason as he is for me.

12

Mason

The following Saturday morning, Sophie shows up at Exotic and Classic Restorations wearing a purple polka-dotted dress and pink striped pants with red snow boots. A sparkling headband completes the outfit. Her coat is unzipped, flapping in the wind. "I'm ready!"

I'm not sure if her multicolored, multipatterned outfit is going to look good on camera, but I can't make her feel bad. I'm sure she dressed herself.

"Great. This'll be fun." I gesture to our director, Hank. "This is Sophie. Star for the day."

Sophie puts a hand on her hip, lifts her chin, and smiles.

May joins us, holding a garment bag. A jolt goes through me the moment our eyes meet. "Hi," she says almost shyly. We saw each other last night at my place, and let's just say May dropped her inhibitions completely. She trusts me now, and I rewarded that trust with mind-blowing orgasms.

"Hello," I say warmly.

She's wearing a tan wool coat, and all I can think about is peeling it off her. I never knew how much better sex is when your feelings run this deep. I want to kiss her so badly, but hold back. We're keeping things private for now.

She clears her throat and speaks in a professional tone. "I

brought several options for outfits. Sophie's wearing her choice of wardrobe."

"Hank?" I ask, figuring he'll be the one to tell Sophie to change.

"The bolder, the better," Hank says.

May sends me a surprised look. I shrug. We both look at Sophie, who smiles, spots Dad, and runs over to talk to him.

"Can she read?" Hank asks.

"Yes," May says. "She's been reading since she was three. I taught her."

"She's really smart," I say, though it's obvious.

"I'll give her the script," Hank says. He gestures her over.

Sophie turns to Dad, and they walk over together. As soon as Sophie gets the script in hand, she reads it. It's short since it's a commercial.

May holds out her hand for the script. "I need to make sure it's okay."

Sophie hands it over.

"Okay, this is fine."

Sophie bounces around the set, checking out the lights and cameras, checking in with the crew and peppering them with questions.

"She's a natural on set," I tell May. "Look how interested she is in everything."

"She's curious. Always has been."

It doesn't take long before we start filming. Dad and I stand in front of a classic white Cadillac Coup de Ville, so you can't see that Sophie's sitting in the driver's seat.

I speak to the camera. "*Hot Finds* returns March twenty-fifth with more classic cars and awesome barn finds."

Dad says his line. "We've got a Mercedes SL 300 Gullwing, a vintage VW Beetle, and an old-school Cadillac Coup de Ville."

We step to the side, and the camera zooms in on Sophie pretend-driving.

Hank counts down three seconds on his fingers, cuing Sophie to get out of the car. We left the door slightly ajar to make it easier for her. She pushes it open and hops out, running up to where Dad and I are standing.

She takes a step forward, puts her hands on her hips, and says right to the camera, "Check out the cars you've wanted to drive since you were a kid."

"Cut," Hank says. "Sophie, you're a natural in front of the camera. Let's try it again. This time when you get out of the car, stand between Parker and Mason."

She salutes him and runs back to the car.

I glance at May, who smiles tightly. Maybe she's worried Sophie will get it in her head to drive again. I assured her there were no keys in this car, and the emergency brake is on.

We do two more takes, and then Hank says, "Let's do one more and keep it loose. Sophie, you say your line and anything else you think will get people to watch the show."

She grins and runs back to the car.

May worries her lower lip. I send her a small nod that I hope says it'll be okay.

We run through it again.

This time Sophie says, "It's the car you've wanted to drive since you were a kid, but your mom wouldn't let you. Watch *Hot Finds*, and you'll be in the driver's seat like me." She runs back to the car and gets in.

"Cut." Hank claps. "Fantastic! Come on out, kid. We're done. Good job."

Sophie runs out, ecstatic. "Can I watch it?"

Hank takes her over to the monitor to watch the different versions we filmed today.

I take May's hand. "See? It went well, and she had a blast."

She puts a hand over her heart. "I had no idea what was going to come out of her mouth when they let her improvise. She recently learned a few curse words from school and thinks it's funny to spring them on me."

I laugh.

May's brows lower in disapproval. "It's not funny. We've

had several talks about it. Every time she curses, she has to do a chore."

"That's what we did when we were kids too. Until we were teens, and then mom said we could talk like normal people. She was just keeping us presentable to adults."

May cocks her head. "You had an interesting upbringing."

"Guess it wasn't like yours."

She shakes her head. "My mom was not cool with curse words. Well, you've met her. She's refined."

I pretend to be offended. "Oh, okay, unlike my mom."

"I wasn't comparing. Mom was a third-grade teacher and big on manners."

I take her hand and kiss it. "I eventually learned manners."

She smiles.

"Thanks for letting Sophie do this. I think it'll be a hit. Who knows, maybe we'll get kids to watch the show too. Never too early to learn about cars."

We look over to find Sophie twirling in her dress. "I'm so happy!" she yells to us.

I catch May's eye, and we smile at each other, both of us happy that Sophie's happy.

May

Sophie's on a high for the rest of the day. Maybe I should find a children's theater for her. It didn't occur to me that she'd love performing. In hindsight, she does love attention, dressing up, and acting out her made-up fairy scenarios.

We're sitting in the living room, waiting for our pizza to be delivered, and she's still talking about how great it was to do a commercial for her favorite show besides *Twinkle Fairies*.

"I'm glad," I say, "but that was a onetime thing."

She sighs. "I know."

"If you want, I can look for a children's theater for you."

She brightens. "What do they do there?"

"The kids act out stories onstage for an audience."

"Do they wear makeup and pick their own costume?"

"I'm not sure. I'll look into it, okay? I'm sure Grandmom would know."

"I'll call her right now." She grabs the phone and presses the button for the contact list I stored in there.

The doorbell rings. Must be the pizza.

I open the door to find Mason holding our pizza box. I freeze. We agreed to keep things private between us.

He smiles. "I saw the delivery guy coming up the walk, so I paid him and said I'd deliver it myself."

"What're you doing here?"

"I have great news, and I couldn't wait to share it. It involves Sophie too. Where is she?"

"She's on the phone in the family room. Tell me first."

I take the pizza into the kitchen, and he follows.

"Don't eat without me!" Sophie yells from the family room. And then loudly into the phone, "Sorry, Grandmom, pizza's here. When you saw *Shrek* at the children's theater, was Fiona wearing green makeup? Cuz I want to wear green makeup."

Mason steps close to me, lowering his voice. "Before she gets in here, Hank sent the promos we filmed today to my aunt Claire. Our show is under her production company. Anyway, Claire loved Sophie's improvised version. She says she has a presence and energy that lights up the screen. She wants her for a movie she's producing and directing. Sophie would play the kid version of the lead."

My hand goes to my throat. "A movie?"

"Aunt Claire says she can get her an agent. It could be the start of a fun hobby for Sophie."

"Or take over her life. You've heard the horror stories of child actors who get into drugs because they don't have a normal childhood."

"Shayla was a child actor, and she turned out great."

"You said she was in the Hollywood party scene as a

teenager. That's why she stayed with your aunt Claire for the summer."

"But she came through fine, and now she's very happy with her career."

I cross my arms. "No. Local children's theater is one thing. Working on set with adults, no school—"

"Claire says it would likely be a week of work. She can miss a week of kindergarten."

"Hi, Mason!" Sophie exclaims, appearing next to us. "Are you having pizza with us? Why am I missing a week of kindergarten?"

Mason looks to me for the answer. Welp, now that she's seen him, it wouldn't hurt to have dinner with him.

"Would you like to stay for pizza?" I ask.

He smiles. "I'd love to."

"Why am I missing a week of kindergarten?" Sophie asks again.

I shake my head. "You're not. Set the table with napkins and plates, please. I need to talk to Mason for a minute."

"Okay."

I pull Mason to the far end of the living room. "Don't mention the movie thing to her. She's not missing any school. I don't want this for her."

"I trust Aunt Claire. You've met her. Nice lady. If she recommends an agent, and she's on set, Sophie will be fine."

"And then what if her agent gets her more work? Next thing you know, she's flying out to LA to film God knows what with strangers, and I'll have to be there too, abandoning the inn. No. Just no."

"You're getting ahead of yourself. This is just for a week. Opportunities like this don't come up that often. And she had fun today."

I see red. He's arguing with me about my own daughter. "You have no say here. She's my daughter, my responsibility. In fact, you should go."

"May, I wasn't trying to—"

"I don't think it's a good idea for you to continue to be around Sophie."

He holds up his palms. "I came on too strong. It's just that I think she'd have a blast."

I clench my teeth. "You're not part of this family."

He steps back, hurt. "I suppose you're right."

My throat tightens because I know this is goodbye. I have to protect Sophie at all costs. Never get between a mother and daughter. "I *am* right."

"That means I'm not part of your life because your family is your life."

I incline my head, the emotion clogged in my throat preventing speech.

"Let me save you the *it's complicated* speech. We should take a break from whatever this is. Get some perspective."

I nod.

He kisses my cheek. "Goodbye, May. Say bye to Sophie for me."

"You can tell her yourself."

"I think it's best if I step away."

I hold my head high, refusing to cry in front of him. I did the right thing. He needs to know I make all decisions concerning Sophie.

The door shuts quietly behind him. I blink back tears.

"Mommy?"

I pull myself together. "Coming."

Did we just break up over a parenting decision?

Mason

I find myself at Happy Endings, where I first met May. It's a busy Saturday night. My cousin Cooper serves me a cold mug of beer, gives me a questioning look, and moves on to his next customers. I guess I look as bad as I feel.

I was just trying to offer something fun for Sophie, and I don't get why May dug her heels in about it. I thought she trusted me. I told her it would be perfectly safe with my aunt Claire in charge. It just seems like I'm in, and then suddenly I'm out in the cold. I want to be all in.

I take a long drink of beer and rest my elbows on the bar top. How do I get past her walls and permanently into her heart? Besides her hair-trigger defenses, everything else about her is perfect. Well, not perfect, but perfect for me. We have fun together. She's beautiful, smart, sweet. She's everything I ever wanted in a woman and didn't know it until I met *her*. The woman for me.

Cooper, with his perpetually ruffled brown hair, returns. He leans down to look at me. "Woman trouble?"

I grunt, embarrassed because I'm here for his help. Whom else could I turn to? My brothers would laugh their asses off. They've never been in love and don't get it. Cooper's engaged to Rowan, and before her, he had several relationships. He's as close to an expert as I'm going to get.

Cooper leans across the bar. "I heard your parents are against a relationship since she has a kid."

"Yeah, but we were working around it." My throat closes, and I take a sip of beer. "I just wasn't done, you know?"

"And she was."

I blow out a breath and tell him the story of Aunt Claire discovering Sophie and May dumping me because I pushed her on it.

"And she said I'm not part of her family," I finish.

"Well, you're not."

A guy signals for more drinks. Cooper holds a finger up to me and sends refills down the other end of the bar. I finish my beer, feeling worse by the second.

As soon as he returns, I say, "Don't you see? Sophie is her life. If I'm not part of her family, then I'm not part of her life."

"And you want to be."

"Yes, but not like…we were taking it slow." *And slow turned into a dead stop.*

"The way I see it, you have two choices—commit to May and Sophie, or walk away."

"Is it too soon?" I wonder out loud.

"Not when you know it's right. When you know in here —" he points to his heart "—that she's the One."

"You sound like your mom." His mom, Aunt Hailey, is a wedding planner and unofficial town matchmaker.

"Mom's a smart lady. May just needs to feel secure in the knowledge that you're not going anywhere. And don't step on her toes when it comes to parenting. She's been in Sophie's life a lot longer than you have. Gotta earn that kind of trust."

"How do you know anything about mothers and kids?"

"I listen. You're not the first person to come to the bar with your tale of woe."

I snort. *Tale of woe.* Then I study him for a moment. He's relaxed and happy. I'm miserable. He knows what he's talking about. But marriage? Being a dad?

"These things can't be rushed!" I exclaim.

He calmly collects nearby glasses and sets them in the sink under the bar. "You don't have to propose, just let her know you're not going anywhere."

I leave the bar mulling over what he said. Where's the line between marriage and I'm not going anywhere? I want to be permanently in her heart, so that means I have to let her permanently into my heart. I'm not sure how to say I'm ready for a commitment. All I can do is try.

I walk back to the inn and ring the bell.

May answers the door, her lips forming an O of surprise. "Mason, I didn't expect to see you."

"I'm sorry for overstepping with parenting stuff. I just thought she'd have fun on a movie—"

She steps on the porch and shuts the door behind her. "Shh, I didn't tell her about that." She tightens her cardigan around her. "Mason, this is on me. I never should've gotten involved with you. It's just not the right time in my life or Sophie's."

My gut churns. "But I like Sophie. She's a great kid. And you and I are good together. We love each other."

She frowns. "One day when you're a parent, you'll understand."

"I'm not going anywhere," I blurt in desperation.

She gives me an apologetic look, turns, and goes inside, the door shutting quietly behind her. Sophie peeks out the front window and waves at me. My heart lurches. I give her a wave, but can't manage a smile.

I turn and walk away. So much for Cooper's advice. May's closed herself off, and there's no getting through that defense system.

Alice takes a sip of coffee and studies me. We're at Something's Brewing Café, where I invited her after a restless night thinking about where things went wrong with May. It's hard to look at Alice because she looks so much like May, except not closed off.

"Thanks for meeting me," I say.

She smiles. "Of course. I sensed from your four a.m. text that it was urgent." She holds up her phone to show me my own embarrassing text: *Need help with May. Screwed up. Urgent.*

"How did you screw up?" she asks gently.

I tell her the story about Sophie and the movie, my later apology, and how May suddenly closed off to me forever.

Alice sips her coffee. "She's a protective mama bear with her cub."

"But I'm okay with seeing each other and leaving Sophie out of it like we did before."

"She probably realized it's impossible to leave Sophie out of any relationship. Sophie's still little and hoping for a daddy."

"I know that, which is why I told May I'm not going anywhere, and she walked away! What would get through her defense system?"

"Ooh, that's a tough one. Honestly, I think she's having a

hard time letting love in because of what she's been through loving and losing her husband. She's only dated once since then, but her heart wasn't in it. When he cheated, it was easy for her to let him go. But *you*, well, you she couldn't resist. The fact that she dated you at all was a huge risk for her, so that's a compliment to you."

"She's sure resisting me now," I grumble.

"Do you love her?"

"Yes. Absolutely. And she said she loves me too." I jam a hand through my hair. "I guess love isn't enough."

Alice gives me a sympathetic look. "It's going to take a lot to get through to her."

"What do you suggest? I'll do whatever it takes."

Alice gets a gleam in her eye and a dangerous smile.

"What?"

"Make a grand gesture! That's what my dad did for my mom to win her over. Legendary! Mom still talks about it."

A legendary grand gesture?

"What did he do?"

She wags her finger at me. "Nuh-uh. His grand gesture came from *his* heart. Yours has to come from *your* heart. Just think about it. I'm sure you'll come up with something fabulous."

"Flowers? Candy? Jewelry?"

She scoffs. "Any guy can do that. Something that says how you *feel*."

While I sit there confused about what kind of gesture shows feeling, she stands with her to-go cup. "Good luck! I'm rooting for you."

"Wait! I still need help."

She gives me an indulgent smile. "Mason, you have every-thing you need right here." She taps her heart.

"Maybe I should talk to your dad."

She laughs. "Good luck with that. He'd prefer if his grand gesture was never mentioned again."

"But it worked."

She shakes her head, still smiling, and walks out the door.

I consider the embarrassment factor of going to May's dad, a guy who's not exactly warm and fuzzy. He'd probably tell his wife, who would say something to May, and then I wouldn't have the element of surprise on my side.

I pull out my phone and search for grand gestures. Hot-air balloon, sky writing, a surprise trip. None of those sound quite right. A trip maybe, but May's opening the inn soon, and then there's Sophie to consider.

The inn. I leap from my seat. I know what to do.

May

I pour peppermint tea and join Alice at the kitchen table. She came over for dinner, saying we needed to talk, and spent most of dinner talking to Sophie. Now that Sophie's playing with her fairy playset in the family room, I can finally find out Alice's news.

I watch her expression carefully, already tense. I prefer not to wait for bad news. "So what's going on?"

She holds up a hand. "No one's sick or dying."

I relax. "Is everything okay with you and Charlie?" That's her husband.

"He's great. I want to talk about Mason."

I instantly shut down. "Anything but him."

"May."

"Alice."

"He's miserable without you."

That gets my attention. "How do you know?"

"I ran into him at Something's Brewing Café. He looked like he hadn't slept in a week."

"It hasn't even been a week yet. We just broke up. Did he tell you what he did, trying to get in between me and Sophie?"

"Yes, and he told me he apologized."

I warm my hands on my teacup. "I have to put Sophie first. I'm all she has."

"Sophie has family—me, Mom, Dad, aunts, uncles, cousins, and Mason, too, if you let him."

I push away from the table and dump my tea in the sink.

Alice joins me at the sink. "He could be worth the risk. Don't push him away."

"You don't have kids," I snap. "You couldn't possibly understand the responsibility I carry."

Her eyes flash. "Sophie is like my own daughter. I loved her before she was born."

I shake my head. "It's not the same. When you have kids, we can have this conversation."

"I'm not having kids. It's a legit life choice. And I'm happy with my life, thank you very much. Can you say the same?"

That stings. "Sophie makes me happy."

"I'm talking about your heart. Love."

"Sophie is my heart."

She sighs. "Sometimes talking to you is like talking to a wall."

"You didn't hear him. He was really pushing to get Sophie into show business, talking about agents and stuff. I wouldn't put it past him to go directly to her over my protests."

"But he didn't do that, did he?"

"Because I ended it. And that's the way it's going to stay. This back-and-forth isn't good for anyone, especially Sophie."

"I thought you kept her out of it."

"I did, but then he showed up unannounced yesterday with his big movie news, holding a pizza. She was thrilled to see him again."

"She's a smart cookie." She squeezes my arm. "I wish you were too."

"I'm as smart as you are."

"Not about the important things." She turns to go.

"Men aren't the answer to everything!"

She turns back. "Of course not. But letting the right man into your life can be a wonderful thing. May, you light up when you talk about Mason, and you glow after you've seen him." She pauses. "Rick would've wanted you to be happy."

My throat closes with emotion.

She kisses my cheek and sails out the door.

I lean against the counter. Love is just too hard. I thought I was ready, but there's too much unknown about the future. Too much risk.

I sink to the floor and cover my face with my hands, letting the tears fall.

13

An hour later, I close my laptop in shock. I call Alice right away. As soon as she answers, I say, "Someone booked the inn for the entire Valentine's Day weekend! I had zero customers, and now I have a full house! Hello? Are you still there?" Valentine's Day is this weekend, and I was so depressed I didn't have a single room booked. I can't believe it.

"Sorry, I'm just shocked," she says. "Who would book the whole inn?"

"Someone who wants privacy. Maybe they're a celebrity or something. I don't know. I just got an email from an assistant."

"That's great!"

"I know! I can't believe it! I've been so worried about recouping costs and getting some cash flow going. There's always unexpected expenses, and I really didn't want to use too much of the life insurance money."

"Huge congrats!"

We say a quick goodbye since I have so much to do. Everything has to be perfect.

I do a little happy dance and get to work gathering linens to make up the guest rooms.

I step into the first room and stop. The urge to share my

good news with Mason is so strong I nearly pull my phone out and call him. But I can't. I lost that right when I pushed him away. I had good reason, but still. I have to live with that decision.

My happiness over the booking dims. I push on, getting the first bed ready.

Once I finish getting the inn ready, I flop on the couch, exhausted. It was pure adrenaline keeping me going. I haven't been sleeping well lately. I miss Mason. The house is quiet for once. Sophie's at a friend's house for a playdate.

The doorbell rings, and I jackknife upright, my heart pounding. I look down at myself in my laundry-day clothes. Oh, who cares? It's not going to be Mason. That's over now.

I answer the door and instantly tense. It's Madison, Mason's mom. I swear if she tells me to stay away from Mason again, I'm going to lose it. I'm already barely hanging on, waiting for these awful feelings of longing and loss to pass. I'm not sure if they ever will.

She takes off her knit hat, her hair askew. "Hi, May, mind if I come in?"

Well, this *is* a very different tone from her last visit. I step back to let her in.

She exhales sharply. "Is Sophie here?"

I cross my arms. "No, she's on a playdate."

"I like her. She's a firecracker."

"Thank you."

She looks around at everything but me. Finally, she says, "I just wanted to apologize for warning you away from Mason. It was wrong of me to come between the two of you. He's a grown man. He knows what he wants."

"Okay," I say slowly. *Did Mason not tell her we broke up?* "Well, thank you for coming. I was just in the middle—"

"It's just that my boy is so miserable now. His dad says he's never seen him so low at work. He's making stupid mistakes; he's got dark circles under his eyes, barely smiles. That's just not Mason."

At my silence, she goes on, "He couldn't stop talking

about you and Sophie. I thought he was just trying to sell my husband and me on the idea, but now I see he was truly happy and in love for probably the first time ever. You're everything I'd want for him. Strong, fiercely protective, and kind. He's told us what a great mom you are to Sophie."

My eyes get hot. "So now you're here to tell me I should be with Mason?"

She speaks in a somber tone. "I'm not here to tell you. I'm here to beg you. I don't know why exactly you broke up, but he loves you. Please. Talk to him. You can work this out. His dad and I will support you as a couple one hundred and ten percent."

I shake my head. "Madison, your interference has had zero effect on our relationship. This has always been between me and Mason. I appreciate your apology, though."

She studies me. "You have dark circles under your eyes too."

"Thank you. Goodbye." I open the door for her.

She sighs and steps outside.

I close the door and cross my arms tightly, hugging myself. It hurts to talk about Mason, hurts to think about him. A tear escapes, and I dash it away. Time will heal this hurt, though I fear I'll never be able to completely get over him. I know from experience that's what love does to you. The person gets into your heart and becomes part of you.

I'm strong. I can deal with this loss. I walk to the sofa and punch a pillow; then I burst into tears. I'm not sure love is ever worth all this pain.

～

Mason

I'm rethinking my grand-gesture plan. It's a huge risk, and if I fall on my face, there will be witnesses. I took off work today to put it all together. Now that it's done, I'm second-guessing myself. I pace around the living room, consider whom I can trust to talk it over with, and the only person who comes to mind is the guy with the legendary grand gesture—May's dad. It worked for him, and his wife still talks about it. I have to know what he did so I know if I went too far.

I ring the bell at his house. It's afternoon, but he's retired. He answers the door in a jogging outfit with AirPods in his ears.

"Hey, Mason, I'm heading out for a run. Liz, May, and Sophie just left to shoe shop for Sophie. It's a team effort for May's sanity."

"I can imagine."

"Sophie has very unusual tastes. You have to be practical for everyday wear." He steps out on the porch, shutting the door behind him. "I'll let May know you stopped by."

He sounds casual. Does he know May and I broke up?

"Actually, I'm here to talk to you."

His brows shoot up. "Me?"

"Yeah."

"Well, come on, let's run and talk."

I don't like running on a nice day, let alone a cold day in February. But what choice do I have? I interrupted his running routine, and I need to know what he did that was so successful.

He starts off at a brisk pace, and I keep up. He runs toward the high school, which is up a hill. Great.

"May told us you broke up," he says.

"Because she wasn't ready to have me in her life with Sophie, but I'm ready for all that. I love her, and I'm ready to commit."

He lifts a brow.

We head up the hill, which is steeper than it looks when you're running. I wish he would say something. Maybe he needs to catch his breath.

Finally, at the top of the hill he says, "Are you asking me for permission to marry my daughter? 'Cause that's something you need to run by her." He heads around behind the school, and I follow. The man isn't even out of breath.

"No, that's not what I wanted to talk about."

Now we're going downhill. Much easier.

"Then what?" he asks.

"I gave May my strong opinion on Sophie being in my aunt's movie, and May completely shut down. She doesn't want me to give any opinion about Sophie, even though I was just trying to say it could be fun, and she could trust my aunt who's producing the movie."

"Heard about that too. She was *pissed*. Guess you learned the hard way to never get between a mom and her daughter. Did you grovel?"

"Uh, I think so. I apologized and explained myself."

He gestures for me to follow. "Let's do the hill loop again. It's a good workout."

I groan inwardly and follow him.

"That's not groveling," he says. "It's when you do something to show where you're at."

"Actions speak louder than words."

"Exactly."

"I heard the grand gesture you made for your wife was legendary. What did you do?"

He actually blushes. "That stays within the family."

"Please, I have this whole thing planned with the inn and Happy Endings, but I'm afraid it's going to blow up in my face. If I just knew what you did, I could see if my idea is too over the top."

He chuckles. "You sound as desperate as I was when I was searching for a grand gesture. The guy I went to was no help at all. I'll do you one better. Here's the secret."

Back up the hill!

He holds up a finger. "One. A gift." He holds up another finger. "Two. Words from the heart. That means a lot to women."

It sounds deceptively simple and much less than what I planned. "What kind of gift?"

"My thing won't work for you. It has to be your thing."

Not helpful!

Great, now I'm getting a cramp in my side. How many uphill runs do we have to do before he tells me what I need to know?

"So you're never going to tell me?" I ask.

"When you're family, you'll know." He winks.

Despite the pain in my body and heart, I smile a little. He hopes I'll be family one day. Now to get May on board. I need to find the perfect gift and the perfect words. How hard can it be?

∼

May

I flop down on the sofa. It's Valentine's Day, and the guests should be arriving soon for their four p.m. check-in time. I'm wearing a floral dress with a cardigan that I hope says professional. Sophie's in an outfit she put together herself that actually works. Okay, yes, she's wearing a rhinestone tiara, but the pink dress, white tights, and black patent leather shoes pull it all together. It could've been much worse, and I wasn't up to a big fight over it.

I spent all week making sure every last detail is perfect. There's nothing more to do but wait for our guests to arrive, and spring into action as the supreme hostess. It's so exciting. When I got the idea to turn my inheritance into an inn last summer, it seemed so far away. And now it's finally happening!

Sophie twirls around the living room, full of energy, even after full-day kindergarten. She throws her arms in the air. "I'm so excited."

"Me too." I consider telling her to save some energy for the guests, but on second thought, it would be good for her to be tired. "Remember, I deal with the guests, and your job is to…"

"Say welcome to the Serenity Inn." She grabs an inn brochure from the plastic holder on the table. "And give them a brochure." She giggles.

"What's so funny?"

She gives me a secret smile that means she's hiding something. Oh no. What if she does something inappropriate with the guests?

"Sophie?"

"I need a juice box!" She runs to the kitchen.

The bell rings, and I jackknife upright. They're half an hour early. I suppose I could let them check in now. Everything's ready. I practice a welcoming smile as I hurry to the door, nearly colliding with Sophie.

"Answer it!" she exclaims. In her excitement, her juice box tips, and juice leaks out on her hand.

"Quick, lick your hand. I don't want juice spilling on the floor."

I pull open the door. Adrenaline fires through me. Mason! He's dressed nice and holding a black plastic case with a red bow on it. Tools?

Sophie claps. "Is that for me?"

"No, it's for your mom. Go get your top three stuffed animals from upstairs to join us, okay?"

She giggles. "Okay."

A trickle of worry seeps in. Does Mason have something to do with her secret smile?

"Did you arrange something with Sophie behind my back?" I demand.

"No, but she knows I have a plan because I told your dad."

My eyes widen. "My dad?"

"Yeah."

I stare at the toolbox and then at him. "What in the world are you talking about? I've got guests coming in half an hour. A full house. Whatever your plan is with that toolbox—"

"May, *I* booked the inn for the weekend. Every room."

"What! Wait, you have an assistant?"

"That was my cousin acting as my assistant."

I stare at him blankly. "Why?"

The corner of his mouth turns up. "It's part of my grand

gesture. You get to start your inn with a bang, and we get to have the whole place to ourselves."

"Mason, we broke up."

"That's why I have this grand gesture, which I hope is legendary."

Oh my God. He talked to Dad about his legendary grand gesture. I'd laugh if I weren't so floored. I thought it was over. I thought it was ruined because of me. But he's trying really hard.

He hands me the black case. I hold it awkwardly. It's heavy.

He flips the latches of the case and opens it to show me. "It's a tire-changing kit and pump, so you and Sophie never have to worry about getting stranded somewhere. See, this is a hydraulic jack to lift the car easily, and the pump reinflates fast. You plug it into a twelve-volt outlet in your car."

I fight back a smile. This is so Mason to give a car accessory as a grand gesture. "Do I have a twelve-volt outlet in my car?"

"Yeah, I'll show you where it is." He points to a tool. "This is a wrench to get the lug nuts off the tire. We can do a test run whenever you want."

I close the case. "Thank you."

His expression turns solemn. "I'm committed to your and Sophie's safety. I want to protect you both."

"That's not—"

"Just listen." He pulls a folded piece of paper from his pocket. He unfolds it and clears his throat. "May, I love complicated. I love you. I'm prepared to commit to you and Sophie. No one will get their heart broken except me if you don't say yes."

My heart's in my throat. *Is he proposing?*

Sophie runs downstairs with a huge armful of stuffed animals. "I couldn't pick my three favorites, so I brought a bunch. What was the present?"

"Mason gave me a tire-changing kit to keep us safe," I say.

"This is from the heart," he says solemnly. "A love poem."

Sophie giggles.

Mason gives her a dark look and continues, "I didn't know what I was missing until I found you, May. When I'm with you, I feel whole, and when I'm not, all I can think about is being with you again. Your beauty, intelligence, kindness..." He glances at Sophie and folds the paper in half. "There's a few other private things I'll tell you later. It would make me the happiest man on earth if you would marry me."

My heart hammers against my chest, the world going out of focus. I think I'm in shock.

14
___

Sophie claps. "Aunt Alice was right! The spark worked!"

Reality returns. "Mason, I-I don't know what to say. I'm so *surprised.*"

He gets down on one knee and holds up a diamond ring. "We can have a long engagement if you want. I just need you to know I'm all in. I love you, May, now and forever. Let me be a part of your and Sophie's life. The two best girls I've ever met."

Sophie beams, and so do I because he's ready to commit to both of us, and that means everything. All the back-and-forth between us was really just me protecting my daughter. Okay, and protecting my own heart too. But I can't resist him anymore.

"Yes!" I exclaim.

"Yay!" Sophie yells.

He slides the ring on my finger, rises, and pulls me into his arms, hugging me tight.

I pull back to look at him. "I love you."

"I love you too. May, you've made me so happy."

Sophie grabs our legs in a tight hug. "I love you too!"

Mason scoops her up. "Are you happy too?"

She grabs his head and stares into his eyes. "Yes!"

He grins. "Okay, then." He sets her on her feet. "I got you a present too." He pulls a small box from his back pocket.

Sophie's eyes shine with excitement as she holds out her hand. He hands it to her. She opens it. "Ooh!" It's a gold necklace with a garnet heart pendant. Her birthstone.

"Every time you put this necklace on, remember that I'll be there for you no matter what."

My eyes well. Mason wraps his arm around me and kisses my temple. This man. This wonderful man.

"Wow," Sophie breathes. She hands me the necklace. "Mommy, put it on me!"

I brush her hair over one shoulder and do the clasp.

"Best Valentine's Day ever!" She hugs his legs and steps back, smiling as she admires her necklace.

I hug him and give him a kiss. "Are you sure you're ready for all this?"

"When I see our future, all I see is happiness."

I go up on tiptoe to whisper in his ear, "Little girls aren't all sunshine. Fair warning."

"Hey, no one is. I'll take my cue from you where Sophie's concerned."

We glance over to where Sophie's standing in front of the window, letting the light catch her garnet gemstone.

I wrap my arms around his neck. "In time, we'll learn how to parent her together. She'll grow and change a lot over the years. I'm so happy to share the journey with you."

He lets out a breath. "I'm so glad you said yes. We can take as much time as you need before we take the next step."

"That sounds good to me."

"Jacket time!" Sophie announces.

I pull away from Mason and watch as Sophie takes her jacket off the hook, puts it on the ground, sticks her arms in the holes and flips it over her head to put it on. They taught her that in kindergarten. She struggles with the zipper.

"Sophie, where do you think you're going?" I ask.

"To the dance."

Mason kisses me on the cheek. "I hoped you'd say yes, so

we're meeting our families at the Clover Park Valentine's Day dance."

"Did you know I've been going to that dance since I was a kid?"

He nods. "Your dad told me. We talked a few times, planning everything. I originally thought we'd go to Happy Endings after I proposed, but the dance is a tradition for your family, so it just seemed right."

"Wow, that was a big risk. What if it didn't go the way you thought?"

"Your dad assured me that with a gift and words from the heart, I couldn't go wrong. That's what he did."

My mouth gapes. "How did you know to ask him about grand gestures?"

"Alice told me he did a legendary grand gesture to win your mom over. She met me for coffee so I could ask her how to win you back."

I shake my head. "I can't believe all this was happening, and no one said a peep. Not even you, Sophie. How did you keep it to yourself?"

She smiles widely. "I get to be flower girl, but only if I was very quiet so you could listen to your heart and say yes. Right, Mason?"

Mason's chest puffs out. "That's right. Your mom needed to hear it from me first." He takes us both in. "Ready for the dance?"

"Yes!" Sophie exclaims. He high-fives her, and they both turn to me expectantly.

"My weekend just opened up thanks to you. I'm still floored that you booked the whole inn and planned all this!"

He grabs my coat from the hook and helps me on with it. "All I can say is thank God you went for it. Ready for the next part of our lives?"

I nod, pure joy bubbling up. I could just float away.

He takes my hand, and Sophie takes the other.

"Ready," Sophie and I say in unison. I can't stop smiling.

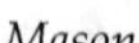

Mason

As soon as I open the door to the dance studio where they hold the dance every year, I lean in and shout, "She said yes!"

A cheer goes up with lots of whistles and hooting too. My family is nuts in the best possible way. I let May and Sophie go in first. The place is decorated with silver and gold streamers and congratulations balloons. Alice planned the decorations for us.

On a small stage beyond the dance floor, a jazz band starts their music. On my right is a buffet table and drink table catered by Happy Endings of course. It's so cool that Happy Endings used to be owned by May's family and then mine. It's fate.

"You guys!" May exclaims, putting a hand over her heart. The new diamond engagement ring sparkles in the light. "I can't believe you planned all this without me knowing!"

Alice joins us. "The key was bribing Sophie." She hands Sophie a cake pop with white icing and a pink heart.

"Best Valentine's Day ever," Sophie says, taking a bite of her cake pop.

"Congratulations!" Alice says, hugging May first and then me. She looks up at me. "I was rooting for you."

"I sure appreciate it."

May's parents come over to congratulate us. Her dad gives me a hearty handshake, leaning in to whisper, "Seems like my advice worked. Congratulations."

I smile. "It did."

"I knew it right from the start," her mom says with a wide smile. "I knew you were right for her and Sophie."

"Thank you," I say.

"Mom, how did you know?" May asks.

She gestures between us. "The way you looked at each other, how good he is with Sophie, and he's easygoing. You have to be to get along with this family. Just look at how he took my surprise visit to his work in stride."

I chuckle. "I definitely felt like I was getting checked out on that visit."

"And you passed." Her mom gives me a hug. "Welcome to the family."

"Thank you."

Her dad jerks his chin at me. "What did you give her?"

May grins. "A tire-changing kit, so me and Sophie will always be safe. It's hydraulic and uses a volt thing in the car."

Her dad hides a smile. "Sounds perfect."

"But is it legendary?" I ask.

"Time will tell," her dad says.

"Oh, I'm always going to remember this gift," May says. "Full of meaning from a car lover's heart."

"That's right." I turn to her dad. "Now that I'm part of the family, what was your legendary grand gesture?"

Her dad grabs two glasses of champagne from a circulating waiter. "Let's have a toast to the happy couple!" he says above the noise of the crowd. He hands a glass to his wife. The band leader hands her dad a wireless microphone.

"Smooth," I say.

"I'll tell you later," May whispers in my ear.

After everyone gets champagne, with sparkling water for Sophie, May's dad lifts his glass. "Liz and I want to welcome Mason to the family. He's shown himself to be a man after my own heart."

"Aww," May's mom says, leaning toward the mike. "I agree! And now we get to have another son."

Not to be outdone, my mom yells, "He's my son!" She drags Dad along with her to stand next to May's parents.

"He'll be your son-in-law," Mom informs them. She lifts her glass for her own toast and gestures for the mike. May's dad hands it over without complaint. "May and Sophie, welcome to our family. And again, sorry about my unexpected chats, May. You get it."

Mackenzie and Harper join Mom and Dad. Mackenzie pulls the mike toward her. "We're also sorry for any weirdness. I hope you liked our apology donuts."

"You're all forgiven!" May yells.

Mom smiles and takes the mike back. "I hope we don't cause more confusion with all the *M* names."

My brothers, Michael, Maddox, and Miles, chuckle.

"Seriously, though," Mom says. "I'm happy for you two, and especially happy for Sophie, who's a girl after my own heart. Never lose that fighting spirit, Sophie."

"I don't fight," Sophie says.

"You have spirit," Mom says. "I'll teach you how to defend yourself so you don't have to fight. I'm a black belt."

"Oh," Sophie says. She runs up to Mom. "Did you see my necklace?" She holds up the heart pendant to show her.

"To May and Mason," Dad says while Mom crouches down to look at Sophie's necklace.

"Cheers!" May's mom says.

"Cheers!" Sophie says.

May and I circulate so I can introduce her to my family, and she can introduce me to hers. She met a lot of them at Shayla and Owen's wedding, but as she says, it was a blur of faces that day. This is the first time I'm meeting her extended family. I was surprised to learn her dad's younger brother married her mom's younger sister. Way to keep it in the family, brothers marrying sisters.

Her uncle Shane and his wife, Rachel, run Shane's Sweets and Something's Brewing Café in town, and Rachel also runs Book It. I've seen them before because of their shops, but didn't realize they were related to May. It makes me wonder why it took so long for May and me to meet since we know a lot of the same people, and I'm in Clover Park regularly.

Aunt Hailey walks over with a tall guy with dark hair and a beard I've never seen before. "Congratulations, you two!" She hugs me and then May. "I knew it from the first moment I saw you together."

"Thank you," I say.

May glances at me, the look in her eyes saying, how did she know?

"She's the Love Junkie," I say.

Aunt Hailey laughs. "Of course I'd love to do your wedding. Just let me know what you want, and I'll make it happen."

"Something small," May and I say in near unison.

"See? A perfect match," Aunt Hailey says. "This is Cal Davis. He's taking over Gabe Reynolds's law practice in town."

While May and I shake his hand, Aunt Hailey gestures for my cousins Mackenzie and Harper to come over.

Mackenzie hugs May. "Congratulations. Again, so sorry for that one time."

"Already forgiven and forgotten," May says.

Harper hugs May. Then both cousins kiss my cheek and congratulate me.

"Mackenzie, Harper, this is Cal Davis, the new lawyer in town," Aunt Hailey says. "He used to be a minor league ball player."

Mackenzie looks Cal up and down with a sparkle in her eye. She likes what she sees. Harper notices and whispers something to Mackenzie, who promptly looks away.

"What position did you play?" I ask Cal.

"Catcher. Too hard on my knees. They got screwed up. Then I went to law school, got some experience in the city, and now I'm ready to run my own practice. I like small towns. I'm from a small town in Minnesota."

Aunt Hailey wags her finger at Mackenzie and Harper. "But don't get any ideas about the new single guy in town. He's a player. Definitely not the marrying type."

Harper holds her palms up and takes a step back. Mackenzie leans in.

"More of a baseball player," Cal mumbles, embarrassed.

"His live-in girlfriend broke up with him for not wanting to commit to marriage," Aunt Hailey adds helpfully. "Well, enjoy yourselves! Come on, Cal. I'll introduce you to more people."

"I can do it, Mom," Mackenzie says with an innocent look.

Aunt Hailey smiles tightly. "I promised to help him get acclimated to his new hometown. We're good. Right, Cal?"

Mackenzie digs her heels in. "I'll get him acquainted with the under-forty crowd since he's clearly under forty."

Cal looks from Mackenzie to Aunt Hailey, unsure what to do.

The music changes to a slow song.

Aunt Hailey sighs dramatically. "Okay, but whatever you do, don't slow dance with him. The last thing I need is my daughter getting drawn in by another player. No offense, Cal."

Cal keeps his mouth shut, nodding once. Guess he doesn't want to get off on the wrong foot with such an influential person in town.

Mackenzie tilts her head at Cal, and he follows her. She stops on the dance floor and wraps her arms around his neck.

Aunt Hailey whirls, facing us with a look of glee. "He's not a player at all. I haven't lost my touch." She turns to Harper. "Now what about you and that nice Nathan?"

"Nice?" Harper echoes, nearly choking on the word.

"Yes," Aunt Hailey says. "Let's get him over here."

Harper points across the room. "Uncle Josh wants to slow dance with you."

Aunt Hailey smooths her hair. "That's the only kind of dance he does. I'd better go. It is Valentine's Day, after all."

She hurries across the room to a surprised-looking Josh. He goes with it, leading her onto the dance floor.

I want a dance with my fiancée. I look over at May scanning the room for Sophie, who's talking excitedly to my cousin Viv. Viv and Sophie tore up the dance floor at Shayla and Owen's wedding. I point Sophie out to May, and she relaxes, wrapping an arm around me and leaning into my side. I tip her chin up and kiss her. We met at just the right time for us. When May was ready to open her heart again, and I was ready to be a husband and father. I didn't think I'd get there so soon, but May and Sophie make it feel right.

"Dance?" I ask.

She nods with a big smile. I take her hand, leading her on to the dance floor, and draw her close, starting a slow sway. She feels so good in my arms, smells so good, too. Desire stirs.

Other couples start to dance around us. Viv and Sophie appear next to us. Viv twirls Sophie left and right.

"Can Viv babysit me tonight?" Sophie asks.

"You're going to Grandmom and Grandpop's house tonight," May says.

"You can babysit me another night," Sophie tells Viv. "Everyone has to take a turn."

"Is that right?" Viv asks, sending me a comical look. I don't think she asked to babysit Sophie.

"She's very popular," I say.

Sophie nods enthusiastically. "I'm thirsty for punch. Come on." She pulls Viv off the dance floor.

May gives me a sexy smile. "A whole weekend to ourselves."

"I reserved the best room at the best inn in town."

"All of this—" she waves around us "—would've been a lot to undo if I hadn't said yes."

"But you did. Anyway, it doesn't count as a grand gesture unless you put everything on the line. That's what your dad said, and it worked for him. He's a smart guy."

We look over at her parents slow dancing and gazing into each other's eyes.

"They're still madly in love after all these years," May says.

"That'll be us at our fiftieth anniversary party and all the anniversaries in between."

She looks at me with love in her eyes. "How soon until we can go back to the inn?"

I smile and pull her close. "I like the way you think. After the cake. I let Sophie pick it out."

"Please tell me it's not *Twinkle Fairies*."

"You'll see."

After our dance, I talk to Cooper about bringing out the

cake early. Hey, it's my engagement night, and I want May all to myself.

A short time later, Cooper pushes the cake out on a cart.

"It's a nine-layer chocolate cake with ganache on top and chocolate shavings," I tell May.

May gasps. "I love it already."

"Sophie said you were a chocoholic."

"Guilty."

I slice a piece and give it to her first. Then Sophie and then myself. Sophie smiles at me adoringly. I could get used to being adored. Girls are so much nicer than boys. My brothers and I were hell on wheels at her age. I'm sure the teenaged-girl hell stories are much exaggerated. I can't imagine Sophie being anything but her sweet self.

I watch as May and Sophie dig in, their faces blissful. Sophie gets chocolate all over her face because she keeps stopping to pick out the chocolate chips on the sides to save for last. Of course, she has to lick each chocolate chip clean first.

When we finish, May looks down at a messy Sophie and sighs.

"I've got her," Mom says, already holding out a wet paper towel. *How did she know?*

She cleans Sophie's face efficiently.

"Let's dance fast!" Sophie does jumping jacks. "Tell the band to play real loud!"

"Sugar high," May says.

Mom shoos us away. "Go enjoy your engagement night at the inn. I'll look after Sophie, as will everyone here. When the sugar crash hits, I'll hand her over to her grandparents. Hey, does this make me a grandmom?"

"That would be wonderful," May says. "Her other grandparents live in Hawaii, so we don't get to see them often."

Sophie attempts a cartwheel and nearly knocks into someone.

Mom smiles. "Finally, I get to be a grandmom. Four grown sons and no grandkids. Good job, Mason."

"It was more May who deserves the credit for Sophie," I say.

"But you won them over. Did you like the tire-changing kit?" she asks May.

"Yes, very nice."

"I have one, too, and it works great. So much better than cranking the jack by hand. It's just *zzziip*. Car up, and you're ready to change or pump the tire depending on your situation. I've learned a lot about cars from my husband. I'm practically a mechanic myself."

I give her a kiss on the cheek. "Bye, Mom. Thanks for looking after Sophie."

Sophie's running in place now.

May smiles. "Yes, thank you."

Mom grabs May in a fierce hug. She lets out a tiny shocked exhale as Mom squeezes the breath from her. Mom leans back and pats May's shoulder. "You can call me Mom. I always thought a daughter would be interesting."

"I'll try to live up to that, Mom," May says.

Mom wipes her eye. "Damn allergies."

"In winter?" I tease.

She narrows her eyes at me and leans down to Sophie. "Let's go ask the band to play fast songs so we can really dance."

Sophie takes Mom's hand and skips along beside her. Now there's a girl with an open heart.

I take May's hand and kiss her palm. "Now it's our time."

She kisses me and turns to the crowd. "Bye, everyone, thank you!"

Everyone keeps talking.

I hit a fork on a glass. "We're leaving. Thank you very much for coming. May and I have a Valentine's reservation at the best inn in town. Serenity Inn is open for business. Spread the word."

May squeezes my arm. "This isn't the time for business."

"We've got to get word-of-mouth going. This is gossip

central, and my family loves to help out people with suggestions."

I scoop her up in my arms and walk out the door with her. She presses her head against my chest, right over my thumping heart.

~

May

My head is spinning from tonight's events. Mason was the celebrity behind booking the inn, an engagement, an engagement party, and now we have the night all to ourselves. It feels like a dream.

When we get back to my house, Mason helps me off with my coat. I turn and smile at him.

He takes off his coat and smiles back. "You look happy."

"I am. I knew I loved you, but some part of me held back." I wrap my arms around his neck. "Not anymore. Mason, I'm all in, body, heart, and soul."

He wraps his arms around my waist. "That is a beautiful thing. I'm honored."

We kiss. A long, lingering kiss that promises more. I take his hand and lead him toward the stairs.

"It feels like forever since we've had alone time," I say. "Translation: naked time."

"Naked works."

He sweeps me off my feet and carries me upstairs. What a romantic!

I stroke the hair at the nape of his neck. "I still can't believe we're engaged."

"Do you want a long engagement?"

"That's not necessary. When it's right, it's right. I'm glad we both want something small."

He sets me down at the top of the stairs and gets serious. "May, if it's okay with you, I'd like to officially adopt Sophie and give her my name. Shaw."

Tears leak out. "That would be wonderful."

"Do you think she'd like that?"

"Are you kidding? You're her dream daddy. She'd love that."

We smile at each other. I turn, about to open the door to my third-floor apartment when he says, "One more question."

"What happened to naked time?"

He takes both my hands in his and kisses them each in turn. That's right, this man takes his time. "I'll make it worth the wait. How do you feel about having a baby with me?"

Butterflies dance in my stomach. I'm surprised but happy. "I always hoped to have three kids."

"I'd like that with you, May. I love you so much."

"I love you too."

He nips my lower lip. "After the wedding. I'm not that kind of guy."

I laugh and kiss him; then he sweeps me off my feet and carries me upstairs once more. I could get used to this.

EPILOGUE

Springtime…

Mason

It's our first episode of *Hot Finds* for the new season, and I'm thrilled to have my two favorite girls on set with me. Our commercial with Sophie in the Cadillac Coupe de Ville did so well we decided to feature the car and Sophie with us in the first episode. May's okay with Sophie being on the show because she trusts me, but that'll be the end of Sophie's show business career until she's eighteen.

"Ready, Sophie?" I ask.

She nods enthusiastically. She's dressed in gray coveralls with her name embroidered on the front and a *Hot Finds* cap just like me and Dad. She is a Shaw, after all. After a small wedding at the inn last month, I legally adopted Sophie.

I direct her to stand next to me. A few moments later, the cameras roll, and I introduce the episode.

"Welcome back to *Hot Finds*. This is a special episode for me because my daughter Sophie's here. She's a chip off the old block."

"Daddy! You're not a block, but you are old." Heat creeps up my neck. That was *not* in the script.

My dad snickers, and the crew holds back laughter. I knew it'd be a risk having Sophie on camera with the way she says exactly what she thinks at all times, but Aunt Claire, our producer, assured me it makes good television.

I turn to May, who's grinning at my embarrassment. "May, come on out here. My beautiful wife, May." Now I'm off script too, 'cause that's the way we roll in this family.

The camera pans to May. She waves it away. Sophie runs over, grabs her mom's hand, and pulls her over to me. Blushing, May gives a small wave, suddenly shy on camera.

Sophie plants her hands on her hips and looks right at the camera. "Sorry, ladies, he's taken by my mom."

This time I laugh. May shakes her head.

Sophie turns to me. "My friend Olivia H. says all your women fans want to marry you, but now it's too late for them."

Camera's still rolling. I can picture Aunt Claire getting a real kick out of this when she sees it later.

"That's right," I tell Sophie with a straight face. "Because I love your mom forever and you too."

"Can we get back to the Cadillac?" Dad asks.

Sophie sighs. "That's what I was about to do, Grandpop!"

And the show goes on, just like my life. Full of the people I love and surprises along the way. We just found out May's pregnant.

Don't miss the next book in the series, *The Fun Part*, where Mackenzie ignores her mom's warning about Cal's player ways only to walk right into Cupid's arrow. Matchmaking mom, Hailey, still has the magic touch!

Sign up for my newsletter to be emailed when *The Fun Part* releases. https://www.kyliegilmore.com/newsletter

P.S. Check out May's parents' story with her dad's legendary grand gesture in the free book *The Opposite of Wild*. Mason's parents have their own hilarious story in *Inviting Trouble*.

ALSO BY KYLIE GILMORE

The Happy Endings in Clover Park series<<2nd generation Happy Endings Book Club love!

The Kissing Part (Book 1)

The Sexy Part (Book 2)

The Sweet Part (Book 3)

The Fun Part (Book 4)

The Tempting Part (Book 5)

Happy Endings Book Club Series <<the Campbell family and a romance book club collide!

Hidden Hollywood (Book 1)

Inviting Trouble (Book 2)

So Revealing (Book 3)

Formal Arrangement (Book 4)

Bad Boy Done Wrong (Book 5)

Mess With Me (Book 6)

Resisting Fate (Book 7)

Chance of Romance (Book 8)

Wicked Flirt (Book 9)

An Inconvenient Plan (Book 10)

A Happy Endings Wedding (Book 11)

The Clover Park Series <<brothers who put family first!

The Opposite of Wild (Book 1)

Daisy Does It All (Book 2)

Bad Taste in Men (Book 3)

Kissing Santa (Book 4)

Restless Harmony (Book 5)

Not My Romeo (Book 6)

Rev Me Up (Book 7)

An Ambitious Engagement (Book 8)

Clutch Player (Book 9)

A Tempting Friendship (Book 10)

Clover Park Bride: Nico and Lily's Wedding

A Valentine's Day Gift (Book 11)

Maggie Meets Her Match (Book 12)

The Clover Park Charmers series <<sweet and sexy charmers!

Almost Over It (Book 1)

Almost Married (Book 2)

Almost Fate (Book 3)

Almost in Love (Book 4)

Almost Romance (Book 5)

Almost Hitched (Book 6)

The Rourkes Series <<swoonworthy princes and kickass princesses!

Royal Catch (Book 1)

Royal Hottie (Book 2)

Royal Darling (Book 3)

Royal Charmer (Book 4)

Royal Player (Book 5)

Royal Shark (Book 6)

Rogue Prince (Book 7)

Rogue Gentleman (Book 8)

Rogue Rascal (Book 9)

Rogue Angel (Book 10)

Rogue Devil (Book 11)

Rogue Beast (Book 12)

Unleashed Romance <<steamy romcoms with dogs!

Fetching (Book 1)

Dashing (Book 2)

Sporting (Book 3)

Toying (Book 4)

Blazing (Book 5)

Chasing (Book 6)

Daring (Book 7)

Leading (Book 8)

Racing (Book 9)

Loving (Book 10)

**Check out my website for the most up-to-date list of my books:
kyliegilmore.com/books**

ABOUT THE AUTHOR

Kylie Gilmore is the *USA Today* bestselling author of over fifty humorous contemporary romances. Her series include Happy Endings in Clover Park, Unleashed Romance, the Rourkes, the Happy Endings Book Club, Clover Park, and Clover Park Charmers. With more than three million downloads of her books, readers all over the world love escaping into her hilarious feel-good romances featuring strong bonds with family, friends, and community.

Kylie lives in New York with her family. When she's not writing, reading hot romance, or dutifully taking notes at writing conferences, you can find her happily crafting what will surely be future family heirlooms.

Sign up for Kylie's Newsletter and get a FREE book! kyliegilmore.com/newsletter

For text alerts on Kylie's new releases, text KYLIE to the number (888) 707-3025. (US only)

For more fun stuff check out Kylie's website https://www.kyliegilmore.com.

www.ingramcontent.com/pod-product-compliance
Lightning Source LLC
Chambersburg PA
CBHW070547100726
47907CB00004B/1307